2.50

D0619067

Goal
Behind The
Curtain

Cliff Rennie

Christian Focus Publications Ltd

ISBN 1 871676 47 9

Published by Christian Focus Publications Ltd.,
Geanies House,
Fearn, Ross-shire,
IV20 1TW,
Scotland, U.K.

Contents

To Martin, Athole and Craig
Three Great Supporters

Sincere thanks to
Mrs. Nessie Rose for the
typing of the manuscript.

CHAPTER 1

A WONDERFUL DAY

'Look! Look, Richard! Over there! I can hardly believe it. That's Doug Mackay, the great football player – and the man who once risked his life to help us in Romania.'

With those words the visitor took his young son eagerly by the arm and hurried across the square in the direction of a man who was standing a little apart from the excited crowd gathering near the large wall, which was almost covered with graffiti.

It was December 1989, and the place was West Berlin. The Berlin Wall had a very special significance for Doug Mackay. Once, years before, under its grim shadow he had dodged death by inches in a dramatic escape from the Communist zone.

'Mikhail! Is it really you? How wonderful to see you again after all those years – and on such a day as this.' Doug beamed as he grasped the man's hand in both of his, before his Scottish reserve succumbed to a Romanian bear-hug.

'Richard,' said Mikhail, turning to his son, 'this is the one I've told you so much about. Long ago, before you were even born, he came to our poor unhappy country to entertain us with his soccer skills. But he also brought something else – the Bible, God's Word. What risks he took for us...'

Mikhail broke off in mid-sentence as a loud cheer went up from the crowd.

'The Wall! The Wall – it's coming down,' shouted a young woman.

'Down with the stones of slavery,' yelled an elderly man.

The bulldozers and cranes from the Communist zone

5

moved sections of the huge stone barrier, revealing ecstatic crowds of East Berliners who poured through the gaps in the wall to embrace friends and loved ones from the West. The air was filled with emotion and the many cries of joy blended into a prolonged cheer of victory.

Doug Mackay smiled and there were tears of joy in his eyes as he saw this, the most hated symbol of Communist oppression, being dismantled.

What a wonderful day!

One after another, the countries of Eastern Europe were overthrowing the oppressive régimes which had closed them off, like an iron curtain, from the rest of the world.

Doug had prayed for such a day as this to dawn. Yet, as he stood there, it was like a dream – almost too wonderful to be true.

As the cheering of the people grew louder, it reminded Doug of that day when, in a sense it all began, the day he made his debut for Dalkirk Albion in a Scottish Premier Division match at their home ground of Brickwell Stadium in Dalkirk, the little town which had stood for centuries at the crossroads of Scottish history.

The memories flooded back through the years. It had all been so strange. He had been only eighteen years old and a student at Stirling University, when he had been approached by the Dalkirk manager, Jim Murray, to sign as an amateur for the Club. Doug had liked football for as long as he could remember. It was a family trait inherited from his father, Rev. Alec Mackay, a Church of Scotland minister, whose calling had brought him from the rugged beauty of the Highlands to the demands of a large parish in the Central Belt. Doug had missed the friendships and adventures of his childhood home, but he had gradually settled in the Lowlands, making new friends and enjoying the increased opportunities to play football. It had been a dream come true when he was asked to sign for Dalkirk.

The atmosphere of a big game is something special, even for the young spectator, but Doug could not have imagined what it would be like to actually take the field against one of the biggest sides in the land – Dalriada of Glasgow, a team with a European reputation. Doug had been chosen as a substitute for that particular match and realised that he could expect to get no more than a short run near the end of the game as one of the regular players tired under the pressure of such a demanding game.

That afternoon flashed through Doug's mind as he recollected the highlights. Brickwell Stadium was packed to its 20,000 capacity and at least half the crowd were Dalriada supporters. The splash of colour on the terracing and the roar of the fans that never quite died away throughout the game were unforgettable. The pre-match tension in the dressing-room, the smell of the wintergreen – these things lived in a young lad's memory.

Doug seemed borne along on a wave of unreality as he watched the match from the dug-out. The pace was frantic and the tackling hard, typical of Scottish football. Doug became so wrapped up in it all that he forgot that he was a substitute and not a supporter. His share in this nerve-tingling drama did not end at the terracing wall: he could go all the way to the pitch itself.

In fact he did go all the way that afternoon and sooner than he expected. The first half was only twenty minutes old when Rob Malloy, Albion's midfield player made a do-or-die tackle on Jim Bremner, Dalriada's classy striker. It wasn't a dirty tackle, but

GOAL BEHIND THE CURTAIN

Bremner was clearly impeded in the penalty-box, and the referee had no choice but to point to the spot. Before the Glasgow club could take the kick, however, Malloy needed treatment from Hector Nicol, Albion's trainer. The midfield man had pulled a leg muscle in making his tackle and it was quickly apparent he would not be able to take any further part in the proceedings.

'Right, son, get your tracksuit off and take Rob's place in the mid-field.' It was Jim Murray and he was talking to Doug. The youngster could hardly believe it. Indeed, he was about to protest that it wasn't yet half-time, but the look on the manager's face suggested this was no time for arguing. Stripping off his tracksuit, the lad hastened on to the pitch, stopping by the linesman only long enough to have his studs checked.

The referee noted the newcomer's name, before striding purposefully towards the penalty spot. At the blast of the ref's whistle, Jim Bremner stepped up and dispatched the penalty expertly into the net. The visitors were one up. During the remainder of the first half Doug battled to get into the game, but the pace was incredible. No wonder part-time players found it tough going in the Premier Division. At last, with half-time approaching, the teenager received a pass in space on the left side of the field, deep in his own half. He set off on a run and Dave Ferguson, Dalriada's international midfield player came quickly to close him down. Employing a trick he'd used a lot in school football, Doug feinted left, then quickly moved right, carrying the ball infield. The ploy worked and Ferguson was left floundering, to the delight of the home fans.

Unfortunately for Doug, Dalriada had more internationals on the field that day, and one of them had moved quickly to block his path. The lad shimmied to avoid the challenge, but the ball was touched away

A WONDERFUL DAY

from him into the path of none other than Jim Bremner, who seemed to be everywhere. The big fellow wheeled round and sent a high ball into the penalty area where the Dalkirk defenders were caught in two minds. In dashed Charlie Simmons, the Glasgow Club's coloured winger to score a brilliant goal.

There was no time to restart the game before the half-time whistle sounded and the teams left the field. Doug couldn't help noticing the contrasting moods at the two ends of the ground. The Dalriada fans were singing with delight, whereas the Dalkirk supporters were silent and glum.

'You're not playing badly', said manager, Jim Murray, as he closed the dressing-room door, 'but you lack the confidence to have a go at them. Don't be afraid of them. You're good enough.' He was addressing the players generally and Doug could see how his inspiring words were serving to lift the morale of the whole team. The pep talk over, Albion got ready to go out for the second half. Doug was last to finish his drink and the other players were already disappearing up the tunnel to the pitch. Instantly, there flashed into his mind words his father had often repeated: 'What a man is on his knees before God that he is and no more'.

Bowing his head, he prayed quietly, 'God, help me to do my best and play my part.' It was a short and simple prayer, but Doug had no doubt he would be heard, for he had grown up in a home where prayers were answered, and he had seen it happen many times in the past. Furthermore, he wasn't asking to win, or seeking an unfair advantage. Rather he was praying against those hostile forces of fear, nervousness and intimidation that can hinder us from doing our best.

As he emerged from the tunnel on to the pitch, Doug's glance met that of Jim Murray. 'Have a go, son.

GOAL BEHIND THE CURTAIN

You're doing fine,' he said. These words, in themselves, seemed like a bit of an answer to Doug's prayer, for he had felt at fault over the loss of the second goal. If the youngster had hoped the second-half might be played at a less hectic pace he was in for a surprise. Time and again he was caught in possession, or found his pass to a colleague cut off. But Jim Murray was a shrewd manager and he had known what he was doing in signing Doug Mackay, for as the game progressed, the youngster's reflexes quickened and he gained that extra fraction of speed. Soon his weaving dribbles and cross-field passes were putting the Dalriada defence under pressure.

One move down the Dalkirk right wing ended with the visiting goalkeeper tipping a shot from striker Bill Dawson over the bar. The resultant corner was not cleared properly and the ball bobbed around the six-yard line. Quick as a flash Doug pounced and thumped it into the net. The game was wide open once again and the play flowed from end to end, with first Dalriada then Albion having the advantage. Then, just when it looked as if Dalkirk were in for another honourable, but costly, defeat, Doug robbed Dave Ferguson in the centre circle and set off towards the visitors' goal. A quick one-two with Bill Dawson took him past two defenders and he was within yards of the penalty-box. Feigning a pass to the left, he twisted in the opposite direction and sped past Johnston, the powerfully-built central defender. Suddenly, the goal was looming up invitingly, but just as Doug drew back his right foot to shoot he felt a sharp pain in his left leg, and he was sent crashing to the ground.

There was no doubt about it, a penalty for Dalkirk. As Doug rubbed his bruised leg, Wallace Thain, Albion's sweeper and captain, stepped up to take the all-important kick. He sent the keeper one way and the ball the other way, to tie the score and give Dalkirk a share of the points. Doug couldn't help noticing that it was Albion's fans who were dancing with delight and the Dalriada end of the ground that had gone quiet.

The whistle blew shortly afterwards and the players made for the dressing-room and a welcome bath. Doug suddenly realised that he was extremely tired. He prided himself on his fitness, but this level of football was far tougher than even he had expected.

'That was tremendous, lads,' enthused Jim Murray. 'A few more results like that and we could make it into Europe next season.'

Europe – the word rang like a bell in Doug's mind. If the team could finish in the top five of the League they would earn a place in the U.E.F.A. (Union of European Football Associations) Cup competition for the following season, with the possibility of trips all over the Continent. Dalkirk had never qualified for Europe before. What an experience that would be.

Just how great an experience it was to be, Doug Mackay could not have imagined at that moment.

CHAPTER 2

MISSIONARY ON STUDS

The months flew by, fully occupied with studies and football, there was so much to learn in the University and it required hard work to keep up with the courses in mathematics and social studies. He wasn't a brilliant student, more of a plodder, and he needed to keep at it to master the subject in hand. This was equally true on the soccer front and for much of his spare time Doug could be seen pounding his way round the athletics track, or practising ball control as he battled to keep his place in Dalkirk's First Team pool.

By the end of the season Albion had qualified for Europe, finishing fifth in the League. The following season they would represent Scotland, along with two other sides, in the U.E.F.A. Cup. It was a real cause for celebration, and a Civic Reception was held for the Club by the District Council, who were always quick to pay tribute to local enterprise and success.

Albion fans waited eagerly to hear who their first-round opponents would be, for there were some great teams in that season's competition, including the legendary Real of Valencia, and the crack Italian side, Morino of Rome, who had recently signed Argentinian star, Cassario, for £3 million. What an occasion it would be if one of these clubs were to grace Brickwell Stadium in a Cup-tie.

Doug was as excited as anyone else as he waited for the draw. Meanwhile, however, something else had made a big impression on him. A man had come to the church to tell the congregation about the missionary work he was doing. It involved praying for people living in communist countries and sending out parcels of good secondhand clothing to help them keep warm in the severe winter conditions prevailing in Eastern Europe.

The thing which challenged Doug most was to hear how deeply the people, living under those harsh regimes, treasured the Bible, which was being all but withheld from them. Very few of them owned a copy and they depended on reading individual pages, sometimes written out by hand, to learn God's Word and find the inspiration it can give. Doug knew how important his Bible was to him, for time and again it had shown him what to do in a difficult situation, or helped him recognise some bad habit developing in his life.

Above all, Doug found the Bible increased his trust in the Lord. It reassured him he was never left alone with nothing but his own inadequate resources to rely on. Be it studies, football or whatever, Doug knew God was with him to help him, and that made him feel both secure and grateful. His father often reminded him that Christians were not better people than unbelievers, only better off, because they had responded in simple faith to God who loves everyone. To be without God, Doug realised, was to be without hope in this world, and to be without the Bible was to be very largely ignorant of what God is like.

Doug longed to help the people living under those atheistic governments and he prayed God would show him what he could do, apart from supporting the clothing and food projects now being run by the church. The answer to his prayers came sooner than he expected, in the unlikely context of the U.E.F.A. Cup first round draw. Albion were to play Prazanof, a team from a small town in Czechoslovakia who, like Dalkirk, had never before appeared in a major European competition.

There was general disappointment in the Scottish town over the draw. These teams from faraway places with strange-sounding names were usually technically efficient and difficult to beat, yet they didn't fire the public's imagination in the way the Latin or German teams could do. Doug shared the general sense of disappointment. Even if chosen to play he might not get the time off University to make such a long journey.

It wasn't until a few nights after the Cup Draw that Doug understood how significant it really was. He had just come home from a busy day at University, having completed an essay that had drifted rather too near the deadline, when his Mum told him that his father wanted to see him upstairs in the study. In the study Doug found his father talking with a man he recognised instantly as the missionary who had so eloquently presented the plight of the Church in communist lands.

'How are you, Mr. Firth?' asked Doug, holding out his hand.

'I'm very well, lad,' replied the missionary. 'I didn't expect to be seeing you again so quickly, but,' turning to Alec Mackay, 'your dad will explain.'

'It's like this, Doug,' said his father. 'Mr. Firth, as you know, is involved in all aspects of the work of mission in communist countries.' Here Mr. Mackay drew a deep breath before continuing. 'That work includes smuggling Bibles across different frontiers. Mr. Firth wonders if you could help in this, as you may be going to Czechoslovakia for the Cup Tie next month.'

'The thing is,' broke in Mr. Firth, 'there is such a hunger for Bibles throughout Eastern Europe our couriers are completely tied up. There is a small congregation we have been hoping to supply Bibles to for some time, but up to now we haven't managed. The town is only ten minutes from Prazanof, where Dalkirk will be playing. It shouldn't be too difficult, although there is always some element of risk.'

Doug was silent. He'd been praying for the opportunity to do something for those Christians suffering such unreasonable deprivation. Yet, now that a tailor-made opportunity was presenting itself he felt nervous and unsure.

'What if I'm caught?' the question was blurted out almost before he noticed.

'I'm trusting they won't search the luggage of a visiting football team too closely,' answered Mr. Firth. 'That would be bad for diplomatic relations. It's a fair likelihood they'll let you through.'

'But what if the lad is found out?' persisted Alec Mackay, with concern in his voice.

'It would be his first offence, and only a small consignment of Bibles is involved. I don't think the authorities would be too harsh with him. Even so, it would mean an overnight stay in prison, maybe even longer.'

'What do you feel, son?' asked Doug's father.

'Scared,' replied the teenager at once. 'It sounds a bit like Daniel going into the lion's den.'

'In a sense that's right,' said Mr. Firth. 'What we need to remember is that Daniel was absolutely safe in that den, because he went there in God's will.'

'I – I'll need to pray about it, Mr. Firth,' replied Doug.

'Thanks very much, lad,' answered the missionary, a sympathetic smile playing on his lips. 'It's not an easy decision, but God will guide you. But remember, not a word to anyone. This must be kept strictly secret.'

That night Doug turned the matter over in his mind, reflecting on how much easier it is to dream about dangerous missions than to actually embark on one. This was for real and, suddenly, the glamour had faded away. As he thought and prayed about the matter, Doug reached for his Bible and opened it at the chapter he was due to read that night. He was reading three chapters of the Bible each day which would enable him to cover the whole Bible in about a year. That night he was reading in the Old Testament, in the 41st chapter of Isaiah.

He read through to verse 10, where he came to the words, 'Fear not for I am with you, be not dismayed for I am your God; I will strengthen you; I will help you; I will uphold you with my victorious right hand.' These words encouraged young Mackay. He almost felt his fear and nervousness ebbing away. Surely God would be with him as he went to serve God's people. Then, almost immediately, doubt stole into his young mind. These words were spoken so long ago – to Jews in foreign captivity. Even if they were true for them then that didn't mean they applied to a young Scot smuggling Bibles into Czechoslovakia, all those centuries later.

The fearfulness returned. What should he do? Doug was wise enough to know he needed more than a sense of duty to undertake what could prove to be a hazardous enterprise. He read on until he reached verse 13 of that 41st chapter, and there he found his answer: 'For I the Lord your God hold your right hand; it is I who say to you, "Fear not, I will help you".'

In that moment doubt was vanquished and faith triumphed. Doug knew he had God's word on the matter and he could go forward confidently, even though the butterflies would no doubt return to trouble his tummy again. Doug shared with his parents the decision he had arrived at and they prayed together before going to bed.

Secretly, Alec Mackay and his wife were far from happy with the prospect of their son taking such a risk, but they were wise enough to know never to come between him and God. They had guided him through childhood and advised him in early youth. Now he must make up his own mind. He was, as his Dad often reminded him, 'old enough to ask God for himself'.

Mr. Firth was delighted with Doug's decision and the two discussed the strategy that would be needed. 'The best plan', suggested Mr. Firth, 'is to take a fairly large sportsbag and fill it with Bibles to within a few grammes of the permitted travel weight. Then cover the Bibles with a shirt, zip up the bag – and pray you aren't searched.'

They talked for about an hour, going over the arrangements for handing over the Bibles and receiving in exchange the clothing Doug would need for his stay, and with which he would fill the sportsbag on the way back. When at last Mr. Firth left, Doug was filled with excitement and longing to be on his way.

By the time the great day came Doug's enthusiasm had been dampened a bit. Permission had been granted to miss classes at the University, but he had received a big social studies assignment with the warning that it must be completed soon after his return from Czechoslovakia. Furthermore, although he was included in the team pool, he couldn't find a place in the starting line-up. The best he could hope for was to be one of the two substitutes who might be used in the game.

Worst of all, Doug was becoming apprehensive about his task as courier. What if things went wrong? What if he was picked up by the Secret Police? Would he be jailed? If he were arrested what might it mean for Dalkirk Albion? These questions nagged at his mind during the flight to Prague Airport, and especially during the long wait before they cleared customs. At last the ordeal was over and Doug found himself on the coach taking the team to Prazanof.

Even in his hotel room he felt uneasy. He was sharing the room with full-back Norrie Harvey, who was already unpacking his clothes by the time Doug arrived. 'Your wardrobe is the one in the corner, chum,' said Norrie, 'better hang up your clothes.'

'Er – yes, in a minute,' replied the teenager. 'I'm going downstairs just now – to the toilet.'

'Why?' asked Norrie.

The question took Doug by surprise and he struggled for an answer. 'What's that?' he asked.

'Why?' repeated Norrie. 'Why go downstairs looking for a toilet, when there's a plush bathroom here?'

'Oh, of course, I'd forgotten.' Doug had been so pre-occupied with his problem he hadn't even noticed the room he was staying in. It was really attractive, decorated in lovely pastel shades, and beautifully furnished. It was an ideal place to spend a couple of days, but, right then, Doug couldn't settle.

To his great relief, Norrie decided to go downstairs to the lounge where he could relax with the rest of the Dalkirk squad. Quickly, Doug reached into his jacket pocket and drew out a small rectangular card, tartan in colour and measuring about six square centimetres. With a piece of 'Bluetack' he carefully stuck the card to the underside of the lintel above the door of his hotel room, looking around carefully as he did so, lest any-one was looking. The card was the prearranged sign by which the room containing the Bibles would be identified.

Doug had done all he had been asked to do and he felt a degree of satisfaction as he set off for the lift, leaving the door of his room unlocked. The youngster would have felt much less satisfied if he could have seen the pair of dark eyes that had been watching him from across the corridor and which were still trained on his hotel room door half-an-hour later when a young man entered carrying a blue sportsbag, and emerged minutes afterwards still carrying the sportsbag. When Doug returned to his room to wash and (hopefully) change for tea he was relieved to find the courier had been. The Bibles were on their way to new and grateful owners, and Doug was reunited with his favourite shirt and the tie which he hadn't seen since Mr. Firth had sent them to Czechoslovakia three weeks before as part of the prearranged plan. Doug removed the tartan card from the lintel of the door, and began to relax. He enjoyed his meal and slept well that night.

Next day, after light training and tactical talks, the Albion players went sight-seeing. Prazanof was a nice little town and the lad bought a few mementos for his parents and friends back home. That night the local football ground was packed to its 30,000 capacity and, as the crowd was close to the pitch, the atmosphere was electric.

Albion were keen to impress on their first European outing, but nothing went right for them and they were two goals behind by half-time. The Czechs, however, were too inexperienced to realise they needed at least two more goals to kill the tie before the return leg. They let Dalkirk off the hook and there were no further goals scored by the time the final whistle sounded. Manager Jim Murray didn't seem too disappointed by the result. 'We can still do it at Brickwell,' he said encouragingly.

Doug hadn't been fielded during the game and felt a bit sad. Though he trusted the manager's reasoning that the Prazanof game hadn't been the best scene for his European debut, he was disappointed, for he favoured the slow, steady build-up of continental football to the hurly-burly of the Premier Division, and he would have loved to play for even part of the game. Indeed, the whole episode seemed to depress his young spirit for a time. He was an honest lad and didn't take naturally to smuggling, and furthermore, not only had he trav-elled all that distance just to *watch* a game of football, but he had to make up the lost study time so that he didn't fall behind in his course. To cap it all, he couldn't breathe a word of his adventures to anyone except his parents who, as always, proved very understanding.

'I've found', said his mum when he returned home, 'that sometimes when I am serving the Lord there come times of disappointment and anticlimax. I've learned to just keep on trusting him, and in due course, God lifts my spirits again and gives me encouragement.'

It was good advice and, sure enough, it proved true, for within a week, Mr. Firth sent Doug a letter telling him how greatly the Bibles had been appreciated by the twenty people who had received them, including, amongst others, a minister who had been praying for a new Bible. Doug was thrilled – and touched. He had seen his Dad's bookshelves, stacked with hundreds of books and he knew how important such books were in the work of the ministry. How hard it must have been for the Czechoslovak pastor to do his work with a Bible that was falling apart. The youngster was so glad he had been able to help – able to be the answer to his own prayers for the persecuted Church behind the Iron Curtain.

CHAPTER 3

A SPECIAL DAY

One of the great compensations of training together
with other soccer players in a team is the friendship that
develops, especially after the training sessions are over.
Competing in a tough league like the Premier Division
is serious work and players need to be able to relax.
Doug enjoyed these informal times. He had a great
sense of humour and could take a joke against himself
as well as indulging in the occasional practical stunt,
such as the time he used a kettle of *cold* water to top up
the boss's coffee cup.

His humour was infectious and it helped the other
players and staff to come to terms with having a
practising Christian in their midst. They saw Doug as
very much one of themselves even though he didn't
drink alcohol, never swore, and refused to play football
on Sunday. It was this last point that was the subject of
discussion in manager Jim Murray's office, following
the Monday night training one particular week.

'I like the lad,' Jim was saying to his assistant, Sam
Barnet, 'but you know the problem. We're a part-time
outfit. The extra training on Sunday morning is so
important to us with the second leg match against
Prazanof coming up. Yet he just won't attend. I respect
his wish to be in church and to keep Sunday special, but
I have to get results.'

'And the thing is,' replied Sam, 'he's an amateur. It's
not as if we can insist.'

'He'll just have to be on the sub's bench again on
Wednesday,' said Jim Murray.

Wednesday was a cold wet day. Doug tried hard to
concentrate on maths that afternoon, but his mind kept
wandering to the match which was now only hours

21

away. He had reconciled himself to being a substitute. He prayed he might get a game. He really fancied a crack at a European side, because they played a much slower game. You had time to dwell on the ball and think more precisely what you were going to do with it. He was finding the Premier League so fast and he was picking up a lot of niggling little injuries.

The weather hadn't improved any by kick-off time. The Brickwell pitch was heavy and would soon be chewed up by the players' feet as they ran and tackled. Sitting on the substitutes' bench, Doug was feeling a bit low. Earlier, in the dressing-room, he had been talking with midfield man, Ron Macleod, Albion's only international player. Doug admired Ron immensely and hoped to be like him one day, but he was bowled over when the star curled his lip and said, 'There's no future for you in football, young Doug. You have too many other interests. If you're going to make the grade, you'll have to give up religion and train on Sundays with the rest of us'. Doug was too surprised to answer.

At that moment there had been a loud rap on the dressing-room door, as the referee summoned the teams, so the conversation was ended. Soon Doug's keen mind was caught up with the action on the field. Prazanof were trapped in their own half of the field as Dalkirk mounted attack after attack. The pace was hectic, but there was little pattern to the play, and Dalkirk's midfield weren't managing to dictate things at all.

When one team is throwing everything forward in attack there is always the danger the other team will break away and score. That was exactly what happened. Les Fernie, Albion's right back, was robbed of the ball on the centre line by a Prazanof player who ran thirty yards before releasing a pass which left the Prazanof centre-forward with the easiest of goals. A stunned silence descended on the 20,000 capacity crowd. Surely now there was no way back for the Scots who needed four goals to win. However, Dalkirk kept attacking and at last got the break they were working so hard for. Tom Pearson, the centre-half, sent a long ball for striker Bill Dawson to chase. The Prazanof defence seemed to have the situation safely in hand, but they had forgotten one important factor – the state of the pitch. Instead of bouncing, the ball simply skidded to a halt and waited invitingly until Bill Dawson thumped it into the net. The crowd went wild with delight and kept up their noisy encouragement right to the half-time whistle.

The second half started at the same furious pace and the Czechs conceded a number of free kicks. Albion were trying hard, but things just were not coming off for them. Suddenly, Jim Murray leaned over to Doug. 'Start limbering up,' he said. The delighted teenager stripped off his blue track-suit and began to run up and down the track. When the ball went into touch, Sam Barnet emerged from the dug-out, holding two numbers aloft, No 13 for the substitute coming on (Doug wasn't superstitious) and No 8 for the player being replaced. A chorus of 'Oohs' and 'Ahhs' went round the ground for No 8 was none other than Ron Macleod. The internationalist was making no impact on the game at all, but he scowled angrily at Doug and barely extended the courtesy handshake to him as they met at the touchline.

Doug soon forgot 'Cleody' as he got stuck into the game. As he suspected, it was much easier than a league game. He would never have dared volunteer the opinion, but felt sure Albion were simply trying too hard. Picking up a loose ball, Doug put his foot on it and waited. The crowd moaned impatiently, but he waited until an opponent came out to meet him from the embattled Czech defence. He drew the defender out till a gap had opened up behind, then quick as a flash, he passed to Les Fernie and darted into the open space behind the defender for the return pass.

Doug held the ball long enough to let Fernie begin a run up the right wing, then he returned the ball to him and jumped over the outstretched legs of a second defender, winkled out of the ruck of white-shirted visitors massed on the edge of their penalty area. Now a real gap was opening up and Doug charged through it to collect Fernie's return pass. Bringing the ball under control with his left foot, he fired a thunderous right-footer into the far corner of the net. Without breaking his run, the lad swerved round the goalkeeper, retrieved the ball and kicked it back to the centre circle, so that the game could be restarted without time being wasted.

The excitement of the fans seemed to be reaching fever pitch as Albion's short-passing broke down the opposing defence, and it was only a matter of time before the third goal came along. Tom Pearson was pulled down on the edge of the eighteen yard. Doug and Rob Malloy stood beside the ball. Then Doug moved up as if to flight in a cross. As he came to the ball he stopped and turned away. It looked as if Doug and Rob had got mixed up.

That was exactly what Prazanof were supposed to think. Quick as a flash Doug turned and swung over a cross. It was inch-perfect and Tom Pearson rose to glide it into the net. Brickwell Stadium erupted. The game was right back in the melting-pot. As the minutes ticked away the whole Prazanof team retreated into defence. Although the scores were equal the Czechs had scored one of their goals away from home. That gave them an advantage. Dalkirk had to score again or they would be out of Europe.

The players were all tiring, even Doug, who had only been on the field half as long as the others. One last effort was required. Albion had a Welshman on their right wing, Taffy Rosser. He was a humorous chap who insisted he had come north for the pleasant weather and the genteel football. Taffy had a great turn of speed. Picking up a pass from Rob Malloy he sprinted past two vain tackles before drilling in a cross. Fred Thomson, Albion's other striker, headed it for goal. His effort beat the keeper only to rebound from the crossbar. As Doug lunged forward to head the rebound, the agile keeper touched the ball away so that it went over the youngster's head. As he was falling, Doug brought up his heel firmly and struck the ball. It flew neatly over his head into the net. What a goal to win a match!

As the final whistle went, Doug could see Jim Murray and Sam Barnett dancing some sort of Highland fling. The whole stadium was alive with celebration. Photographers from Edinburgh and Glasgow, as well as from the Dalkirk Courier gathered round snapping the players, especially Doug who was the hero of the hour.

In the dressing-room, Jim Murray wisely let the enthusiasm run its course before speaking. 'You did very well, boys. At half-time I really thought we were finished. It was a great lesson in holding on. As the man said, "It ain't over till it's over". Something else I took on board tonight,' added the manager, smiling broadly at Doug, 'that is *the end* as far as Sunday training is concerned.'

As Doug made his way home alone that night he was deep in silent conversation.

'Thank you, Lord, for giving me a game and for helping me do my best. Above all, thank you for showing the manager and team that it pays to do things your way and keep Sunday special.'

The days that followed tested Doug's character more than anything he had ever known. Everywhere people were coming up to congratulate him – students, even lecturers, passengers on the train, folk on the street. Even the press, ever eager to uncover a new soccer start, were giving him a big write-up.

Doug was glad that, at such times, he could tell his parents how he felt. For a young man brought up to follow Jesus Christ in humility and faith all this adulation and ballyhoo was a bit unsettling. 'Remember, son,' said his dad, 'our Lord never places us on a pedestal because he doesn't want us to fall and get hurt. Instead, he yokes us to himself and bids us follow him. Jesus was often with crowds of people, but he never let them dominate him or deceive him. His whole ambition was to please God. Make that your ambition, lad, and the crowds may hurt you, but they'll never be able to really harm you.'

That evening Doug was a guest at a Supporters' Club social, for the supporters of the Clarewood Branch had chosen Doug as their most promising young player of the previous season. Doug had never attended a Supporters' Club before, and he was in for a number of surprises. First of all, everyone, except Doug, was wearing the blue and gold of Dalkirk Albion. There were scarves, ties, caps and leisure shirts in the club's colours.

The second thing that surprised Doug was to see how many of the supporters were women and teenage girls. They wore blouses and cardigans in blue and gold, and one girl even had a coat in the club colours.

The biggest surprise of all for the lad was the actual presentation. He was given an enormous teddy-bear, decked in Albion hat and scarf. Even funnier than the gift was the fact that the person chosen to hand it over to him was a rather overweight man who looked not entirely unlike the creature he was presenting. The formal part of the evening over, Doug was then treated to a buffet meal. The food was scrumptious and it banished the rigours of training from the lad's mind.

It was a great evening, and marked the beginning of a super rapport with the fans. Unfortunately, however, no-one thought to give the hero a run home, so there was nothing for it but to join the bus queue with his newly-acquired bear. Of all nations, the British are decidedly the best at hiding intense curiosity behind a mask of disinterest. Nobody in the queue spoke to Doug, smiled at him, or even favoured him with a furtive glance. After all, he might be dangerous.

Only when safely aboard the bus did the motley collection of men and women allow full rein to their curiosity. They stared and stared as Doug, red-faced with embarrassment, paid his fare to the suspicious driver. Worse was to follow, for evidently not all children like teddy-bears. Doug sat down in front of a mother and daughter. The little girl, who was about three years old, took an instant dislike to Ted, or Doug, or both, and began to howl the bus down. Doug apologised to the mother and got up to look for another seat.

Walking a full-sized teddy along the aisle of a No 41 bus while it is rounding a bend in the road is an acquired skill – which Doug had not yet acquired. First, the bear catapulted into the lap of a rather severe-looking woman, then Doug lost his balance and landed on the knee of a skinhead.

The bus shuddered to a halt. 'Right, Jimmy,' yelled the driver. 'Get aff ma bus, an' take yer dolly wi' ye.'

'Ho, ho, Mackay, that's a red card for you,' chortled a man at the back of the bus. 'Fancy being ordered off for tackling a bear.'

Although he still had a mile to walk home, Doug was relieved to be off the bus. The laugh had been very much on him and although he could take a joke against himself well enough he didn't like to be a nuisance to people.

However, he and his new 'Friend' were to prove a nuisance once more before they finally got home that night. Doug was passing a large house when he heard the sound of breaking glass. He could see two young lads forcing an entry to the house and shouted loudly, 'Hey, get out of it, you thieves. Get out of it.' The would-be robbers saw Doug, though they did not recognise him, but they were pretty sure they recognised his companion.

'It's Hesperus the Bear,' cried one of them in terrified confusion and the two disappeared like greased lightning.

Doug went straight to the Police Station and reported the matter to a rather suspicious sergeant. 'Now, you wouldn't be having me on, young Mackay? I know you've got a funny sense of humour.' Eventually, the sergeant went to check out Doug's story, leaving one very weary student to carry his teddy-bear home to bed. As he set him down in a corner of his room he couldn't help laughing at the night's events. 'Hesperus Mackay, that's your name, pal – *AND* it serves you right,' he grinned.

Some days later, Doug learned that Dalkirk Albion had drawn the strong Romanian team A.C. Wallachia in the next round of the U.E.F.A. Cup, with the first match abroad. Imagine that! Another trip behind the Iron Curtain, thought Doug. He found himself praying that God would show him if he should try to smuggle Bibles into Romania as he had into Czechoslovakia.

When he got home that night Doug found Mr. Firth,

the missionary, speaking with his dad. 'This is a tougher one, Doug,' warned Mr. Firth. 'There is strong persecution of the Church in Romania. At the same time, it has to be said God is really at work there.'

When he saw how keen Doug was to help, Mr. Firth only wished that more Bibles could be smuggled into the country than the twenty or thirty that would fit into a sportsbag. They talked well into the night, examining all the possibilities, but couldn't see any way round the problem.

'There's only one thing we can do in a situation like this,' said Alec Mackay. 'We've got to ask the Lord to show us his way of getting all those Bibles into Romania.'

They each prayed briefly. Doug's father had seen very difficult problems yield to the power of prayer. As they got up to leave, Mr. Firth congratulated Doug on his recent performances for the Albion.

'Oh, let me show you something,' said Doug, hurrying into his study to reappear with Hesperus. 'Isn't he a fine fellow?' Doug began to recount his experiences with the teddy-bear, when Mr. Firth broke in excitedly, 'That's it.'

'Do you mean you've seen Hesperus before?' asked Doug with a laugh.

'That's the answer to our prayers,' persisted Mr. Firth. 'That bear would hold a hundred Bibles, no bother.'

'Yes, of course,' smiled Alec Mackay. 'And the communist authorities are hardly likely to search the team mascot.'

They examined Hesperus carefully. His head came off, revealing a hollow 'carcase', which could easily be filled with light-weight Bibles. Hesperus was going to come in handy after all.

CHAPTER 4

HESPERUS HEADS EAST

The Rev. Alec Mackay was a quiet man. He worked quietly and effectively among the various people who made up his busy parish near Dalkirk. He had taught his son, Doug, many practical lessons which had proved to be helpful, even invaluable, over the years. He was not a man to hide his faith in a corner. He was not ashamed of the power of God, and often reminded Doug of Jesus' words, 'Let your light so shine before men that they will see your good deeds and give glory to your heavenly Father'.

'Remember, laddie,' he would say, 'your faith is seen by your good deeds not by your fine words. *Let your light shine.* Don't hide it – but don't flash it either. Some Christians can sound pompous and patronising.'

Doug had always tried to follow that advice and he had found that people got the message clearly enough that he took Christ's teaching seriously. Not everybody liked this and one person in particular who found Doug's quiet faithfulness a real challenge to his own lifestyle was Simon Barrie, who played goal-keeper for Dalkirk Albion.

Simon was a communist who believed in the teachings of Karl Marx. Nations like China, Cuba and Russia base their political systems on Marx's teaching and are called communist countries. Doug and Simon often had discussions following training sessions but in the end they always had to agree to differ. At the first training session following the draw for the U.E.F.A. Cup, all the talk in the dressing-room was about the trip to Romania. A.C. Wallachia were a good side, one of the best in the Eastern Bloc and the Albion players knew they would find it very difficult to beat them.

'Never mind,' laughed Simon Barrie, 'Doug's taking a secret weapon to Romania.' He was pointing to Hesperus, the teddy-bear, which Doug had placed in the corner of the dressing-room.

'That's right,' smiled Doug. 'I thought he'd make a good substitute goalkeeper if Simon went over to the Romanians.'

'He's a big chap', grinned Sam Barnet, 'and we'll certainly need all the help we can get. It will take a great effort to win this tie. As they say, we'll need to give it our best shot.'

The weeks rolled on and at last it was time for the trip to Romania. Doug packed his sportsbag with the clothing he would need, and Mr. Firth packed Hesperus the Bear – with Bibles, nearly a hundred in all. Doug was pleasantly surprised to find that the teddy wasn't too heavy to carry, only awkward, and wasn't likely to attract undue attention. Provided airport officials didn't search Hesperus, things should be all right.

When the day of the flight came Hesperus festooned in blue and gold ribbons was packed in with the luggage, where he remained until the plane touched down in Romania. Then the fun and games began.

'Vot is dat,' barked the customs official.

'It's the team mascot,' replied the teenager.

'It iz very big,' persisted the official.

'It has to be,' said Doug mischievously. 'It's going to stop Mihal Calinescu.'

The official obviously recognised the name of A.C. Wallachia's star striker and smiled. 'We beat you eezy – three goals. Ah! Vot iz in de bag?' Incredibly, the man passed over the teddy and instead searched Doug's sportsbag, making cracks about whisky smugglers as he rummaged amongst the clothes.

GOAL BEHIND THE CURTAIN

Later Doug sighed with relief as he slumped into the large, comfortable armchair in his hotel room. The players all had fairly small individual rooms which was perfect for the purpose of passing on the Bibles to the contact person.

Presently a knock came to the door of his hotel room, and Doug opened it to find two men in working clothes. One of them was carrying a plunger and Doug assumed they must be plumbers come to repair pipes. Once inside, however, one of the men turned to him and asked in flawless English, 'Are you Doug Mackay, the friend of Mr. Firth?'

'Yes,' replied the lad in surprise. 'But who are you?'

'I am Mikhail, the minister of a small church in the city and my friend is a member of another fellowship of similar size. We have not registered our congregations with the authorities, because we fear our members could be persecuted. Mr. Firth said you would bring us Bibles. He gave us this card as a means of identification.' With this the man handed over the tartan card Doug had used on his previous Bible-smuggling mission to Prazanof. It was the agreed sign and Doug knew the men were genuine.

Doug locked the door, pulled the curtains and put on the light. It was wise to take precautions. 'The Bibles are here,' he said, pointing to Hesperus. The two men smiled broadly, which pleased Doug greatly, for they had been so tight-lipped and serious, they made him nervous.

'We wondered how anyone could smuggle a hundred Bibles into our country, but now we know. This is a wonderful idea.'

When they saw the Bibles the men were so happy they cried openly. Both men had been using very old, worn Bibles and they really needed new ones. Most members of their congregations didn't own a Bible at all.

Doug had often been moved emotionally as he saw the delight on the faces of Albion fans when their team scored. Part of the thrill you got from putting the ball in the net was seeing the pleasure on the men's faces; but this was different. God's Word was so important to these two men that Doug felt privileged to be the one to bring it to them. There were so many Bibles the men had to make two trips to their waiting van. Before they finally left his room, they prayed with Doug, then embraced him.

The teenager felt good. As he looked back on the year he had been playing in league football, he was astonished to see how God had been with him. He had learned so much, and enjoyed learning it. But there was another lesson awaiting the young lad, one that would not be so pleasant, for as the two men left Doug's room someone was watching, the same someone who had seen the visitor to Doug's room in Prazanof. 'You're up to something, Doug Mackay,' muttered the unseen witness to himself, 'and I bet I know what it is – smuggling. Well, we can put a stop to that.'

It was a mild evening for October when the teams took the field in Wallachia. In front of a crowd of 35,000, the home side proved to be as good as the reports had said and only desperate defensive work kept them at bay till half-time. Simon Barrie was the hero of the first half with some outstanding saves, including a point-blank effort from five yards which left his hands stinging until the teams came out for the second half.

Wallachia's pressure had to tell, and at last it did, with only fifteen minutes left. Mihal Calinescu, who had posed all sorts of problems for the Albion defence, slipped his marker and gave Barrie no chance with a firmly-struck grounder that stuck in the corner of the net. Minutes later, the same player made it two nil, following a mix-up in Albion's defence. Suddenly, from being hopeful, the situation began to look desperate, as the Romanians piled on the pressure in search of a third goal that would surely kill the tie for the Scots. As they pushed players into the Dalkirk half, however, they left their own defence exposed and that proved to be their undoing. Striker Bill Dawson picked up a clearance from Les Fernie and swung the ball out to the right, where Taffy Rosser controlled it quickly before turning inside the left-back. A sudden burst of speed took him past the sweeper and from an acute angle on the right wing he fired in a great shot that beat the keeper completely.

The transformation in the two teams was dramatic. The Romanians lost confidence and went back into a defensive shell while Dalkirk attacked looking for the equaliser. It was the home side who looked relieved to hear the final whistle, and Jim Murray congratulated his team on playing so well. There was every reason to believe they would qualify for the next round by beating Wallachia in a fortnight's time in Dalkirk.

That night the Albion squad were guests at a reception in Wallachia's Town Hall, a relaxing evening which they all thoroughly enjoyed, before returning to their hotel for a well-earned sleep before their flight home next morning.

But there was to be no rest for Doug that night, for as soon as he entered his room he saw there had been visitors. Drawers were left open, clothing was strewn on the floor and the mattress had been closely examined. Somebody had been looking for something. The lad's first thought was that the two church leaders had returned during his absence. Yet, what could they have wanted? Surely they wouldn't leave a mess like this. Perhaps it was just a burglar who had been frustrated by finding nothing of value. On the other hand – the thought struck Doug, what if it was the Romanian police who were responsible? Doug broke into a cold sweat. Had they arrested the Bible men? Had the men talked, incriminating Doug? If they had, Doug felt sure they had only done so as a result of torture. TORTURE! What if he were tortured?

Doug felt the room almost swimming before his eyes, so strong was the panic that seized him. He longed to speak to his parents, but they were hundreds of miles away. So was Mr. Firth. He couldn't talk to his team mates. Oh! Was there *no-one* to listen? Why had he ever got involved in this dangerous enterprise? Then it came to him he had become involved because he was sure God wanted him to do it. He had prayed about it and he'd been in no doubt it was the right thing to do. So why was he scared now?

Doug knelt down at the side of his bed and began to pray. 'Lord, you have promised never to fail those who trust in you. Well, I am trusting you. I have taken the Bibles to your people because you want me to, and if I'm in any danger, I pray that you will help me.'

As the lad rose to his feet he still felt frightened but no longer in a state of panic. He was now confident that God was with him. It was almost as if the Lord had said, 'Hey, wait a minute, Doug, haven't you forgotten something? No need to be alarmed, for I'm still here.'

It was with a sense of relief that he got ready for bed. After such an eventful day he needed a sleep. It took a while for him to fall asleep with so many thoughts chasing around in his mind, but at last he must have dropped off.

How long he'd been asleep he didn't know, but he was wakened by a noise at the door of his room. Who could it be? Was it one of the team coming to check that he was all right? He was just going to shout when he heard strange voices speaking in heavy foreign accents. Then he heard a sound that made his blood run cold. He hadn't heard that sound for years, not since he'd been a boy in the Highlands watching a deer-hunting party go into action. It was the sound of a trigger being pulled back to prime a gun for action.

Doug's throat was dry, his tongue was almost sticking to the roof of his mouth. He heard the sound of a key being turned in the lock, then slowly the door was swung open.

CHAPTER 5

THE PENALTY

In the darkness Doug could not tell who had entered his room, but he was not left in doubt for long. The light clicked on to reveal two men in police uniforms, each holding a pistol which was pointing at Doug. 'Get dressed!' rapped one of them, a tall, lean-featured man whose face looked as if it hadn't worn a smile for years.

'Would you mind telling me why?' asked Doug.

'The Chief wants to ask you some questions,' cut in the other man, tossing Doug's shirt to him impatiently.

Doug dressed quickly. There seemed to be no point in arguing with these men who might be as happy to bring him to their Chief dead as alive. Once dressed he was hurried to a room on the same floor as his own, which had obviously been taken over for Doug's meeting with 'the Chief'. There was a bed there that had recently been slept in and a suitcase on the floor. Dominating the scene was a tall, athletic-looking man with a black moustache. He was dressed in the uniform of a senior police officer. Grim-faced, he handed some photographs to the youngster. 'Look at these,' he said firmly.

Doug looked at the photographs which showed young people in various states of distress. Some had been photographed in bed, others in the street. Doug found them very upsetting and returned them to the Chief. 'Look at them!' barked the man. 'Are they not a pretty sight?'

'No', answered Doug, 'they are not. Why did you haul me out of bed to look at this?'

The Chief looked at Doug and his eyes were full of anger. 'These people in the photographs are from your so-called free West. Once they were healthy boys and girls, as well to be seen as you or me. Now look at them. Their lives are ruined – by drugs.' The Chief went on, 'We don't have a problem like that here in Romania and we want to keep it that way.'

'What exactly has this got to do with me?' asked Doug.

'As if you don't know,' barked the Chief contemptuously. 'We have been informed that you smuggled a quantity of heroin into this country.'

'Whoever told you that is a liar,' said Doug emphatically.

The Chief and his men were taken aback by the sharpness and clarity of the youngster's reply. Only someone with a very clear sense of right and wrong, truth and falsehood, would be so emphatic and fearless in his answer. These officials were not used to dealing with people like that.

'Were you not visited by two men in your hotel room today?' asked the Chief in a more subdued tone. Doug hesitated for a moment, then laughed.

'Yes, there were two men in my room,' agreed Doug. 'But surely, whoever reported them to you must have told you what they were carrying?'

'What were they carrying?' asked the Police Chief, who was beginning to wish he had left the teenager in his bed.

'Plumbers' tool bags and one of them carried a plunger. You know, the sort of thing you clear sinks with.' Doug got up and went through the motions of a plumber clearing a sink.

'All right, all right,' interrupted the Chief wearily, with a dismissive movement of his hand. 'I have obviously been misinformed. My apologies for disturbing your rest.'

Back in his hotel room, Doug again sank to his knees

in prayer. 'Thank you, Lord,' he said. 'As always you have been with me to deliver me. I can always trust you.'

The flight home to Dalkirk was uneventful apart from a small incident which nearly cost Doug his furry friend, Hesperus. A little girl at the airport took such a shine to the bear that she wanted to have it. Her dad, a wealthy North American, was ready to offer a large sum of money for it until Doug told him it was a special gift of sentimental value. 'Tell you what I'll do. The little girl can cuddle Hesperus and have her photo taken with him.' That seemed to do the trick and the big bear was rescued. 'That's another fine mess you almost got me into,' said Doug mockingly.

With Hesperus packed away in the luggage compartment, Doug settled down to enjoy the flight home. He sat beside his pal, Norrie Harvey, who played left-back for Albion, and they talked about the previous night's match as they reclined on their seats. Norrie was from the Manchester area and had joined Dalkirk about the same time as Doug. He had an infectious sense of humour and a funny way of telling a story which made him highly popular with the whole squad.

'A funny thing happened to me on my way to dreamland last night,' said Norrie. 'There was a knock on my door and when I answered it there was the manager and a couple of policemen. The manager asked me if I'd be kind enough to move downstairs to another room. I supposed it was their way of carting me off to jail for snoring too loudly, but being an obliging sort of chap I agreed to go. Well, you should have seen the room they gave me. It was really plush, far nicer than the one I'd been in, and there was a cup of tea all ready waiting for me. And it really happened, I wasn't dreaming.'

Doug listened with interest. 'Where was your

original room?' he asked.

As Norrie described it, Doug realised that was where he had been questioned. The police had obviously made sure Doug had as little opportunity as possible to make a noise or raise the alarm, by taking him to a nearby room on the same floor. But why move him at all? Could they not have spoken with him in his own room? Even as he thought of it the teenager realised what the answer must be. They were moving him to another room to disorientate him in preparation for a long interrogation. He almost shuddered as he thought of it, but decided he could not share with Norrie the experience of the previous evening. That would have to wait until he got home and saw his father and Mr. Firth.

They, for their part, were so relieved that all had worked out well, in spite of the very real fright Doug had had. 'Our contacts in Wallachia are deeply grateful for your help. The Bibles are really appreciated and are being read by their new owners,' said Mr Firth. 'The thing that stumps me is why the authorities suspected you of smuggling drugs, or even heard of your visit from Mikhail and Alexandre. Have you dropped a hint of what you're doing to anyone else at all?'

'No-one knows apart from me, other than Mum and Dad and yourself,' replied Doug.

The mystery remained unsolved and, in any case, the teenager soon had other things to attend to, not least the preparation for the visit of A.C. Wallachia. Albion's performance in the first leg had ensured another capacity crowd at Brickwell Stadium for the second game. With all their players fit, Albion were able to name a full-strength side as follows.

Simon Barrie, in goal; Les Fernie, right-back; Norrie Harvey, left-back; Tom Pearson, centre-half; Wallace Thain, sweeper and captain; at right midfield was Ron

THE PENALTY

Macleod; centre midfield, Doug Mackay; left midfield, Rob Malloy; on the right wing was Taffy Rosser and the two strikers were Bill Dawson and Fred Thomson.

The television cameras didn't often come to Brickwell but they were in place that chill November evening as the teams emerged on to the field to thunderous applause. Dalkirk won the toss and decided to play with the breeze at their back in the first half.

As Dalkirk anticipated, the Romanians had come to defend their one-goal lead and it took the home side over forty minutes to penetrate their defence. When at last the goal did come, however, it was a beauty and well worth waiting for. Norrie Harvey made ground on the left before picking out Ron Macleod with a crossfield pass. The international midfielder took a few steps and crashed a thirty-yard drive high over the keeper's head and into the net.

The crowd was still buzzing with excitement over the goal when the teams emerged for the second half, but their joy was short-lived as Wallachia set about reducing the deficit. They showed some silky skills as they repeatedly stretched the Scots' defence. At last with twenty minutes left to play they scored the equaliser their play so richly merited. Dalkirk failed to clear a corner from the right, and that man Calinescu, with his back to goal, back-heeled the ball into the net.

Albion threw everything into attack for those last twenty minutes for the goal that would push the tie into extra time. No-one worked harder than lion-hearted Bill Dawson who had chased every through-ball without receiving much encouragement. With the minutes ticking away Bill gave chase to a pass from Rob Malloy. It seemed a lost cause, with the ball running away from him at the corner, but Bill's determination was rewarded, for the ball hit the corner flag and bounced back, remaining in play. Dawson dribbled along the touchline, swerved inside a tackle from one defender, drew another out of position, then passed the ball inside to the better-placed Fred Thomson who slammed it past the helpless goalie.

Extra time produced no change in the score, and the game had to be decided on penalties, with each side taking five penalties. If they were still equal thereafter, the two sides took more penalties till one or other missed and thus lost the game. It had been a hard march, lasting 120 minutes in all and Doug felt relieved that he was unlikely to be called upon to take a penalty. Kicking penalties had never been his strong point and he was ninth in order of kicking, ahead of Les Fernie and Simon Barrie.

Each side missed one of their first five penalties, so the competition went into the phase known as 'sudden death'.

Eric Cassidy, a young Irish player, had come on as a substitute for Bill Dawson, who had been too exhausted to complete the period of extra time. Eric took Albion's sixth penalty and coolly placed it into the net with his left foot. The Romanians equalised. Then Norrie Harvey shot straight at Wallachia's 'keeper with the seventh penalty. A goal for the Romanians now would finish it. Doug felt sorry for his pal, Norrie, who was looking thoroughly miserable.

To the delight of Albion's fans, Wallachia's seventh penalty rebounded off the bar, leaving the teams even at five penalties all. Now it was Taffy Rosser's turn. He'd had a great game and seemed to be celebrating his selection for the Welsh international side. Surely Taffy would clinch it. But no! His firmly-struck shot bounced back off the post. Doug could hardly bear to look as the Romanian right-back stepped up to the spot, but the players' nerves were really on edge now and this penalty flew harmlessly over the bar and into

THE PENALTY

the delighted crowd.

Now it was Doug's turn. No longer was he filled with pity for Norrie and Taff. Instead he was thinking about himself. He felt sure he would miss. Then, as he was placing the ball, he remembered his spiritual birthright as a Christian – prayer. Walking back quietly he asked God to calm his nerves and ease the tension. He turned, heard the whistle and fired a right-foot shot low to the keeper's right hand. The ball eluded the man's grasp, struck the inside of the post and cannoned into the net. The roar of the crowd had scarcely subsided when one of Wallachia's midfield players began his run for their ninth penalty. He struck the ball fiercely, but Simon Barrie had guessed correctly where it was going. Throwing himself high to his left, he finger-tipped the ball over the bar. Albion were through to the next round.

The twenty thousand fans sounded more like two hundred thousand as they cheered their heroes to the echo. In the dressing-room the lads were weary, but happy. They had known all along it would be a hard task, but only now that it was all over did they realise just how difficult. Doug felt a lot of sympathy for the Romanians. They had played well and only a penalty had put them out of the Cup. Now they faced a long, lonely journey home. The words enshrined on the motto of an American University flashed into Doug's mind: '*In the dust of defeat as well as in the laurels of victory there is honour to be won – if one has done one's best.*'

Rising quietly from the bench he was sitting on, Doug slipped unnoticed out of the dressing-room, and knocked on the door of the visitors' changing-room. The door was opened by a gloomy-looking official who brightened when he saw Doug's outstretched hand. Doug thanked them all for the game and wished them well on their journey home, and for the rest of their soccer season in the Romanian league. The Romanian manager came over and thanked Doug for his interest. 'We think you can win this trophy,' he said. 'Your team is well balanced and brave.'

As the youngster turned to go back to his own team's dressing-room, the youngest member of the Romanian party followed him.

'Excuse me,' he said. 'You scored the winning goal.'

'That's right,' nodded Doug.

'I think you prayed before you took that penalty.'

Doug was shocked, but delighted, to hear the boy say this, for he was a boy of no more than fifteen, and was probably in charge of the team's kit.

'I too pray and have done so since childhood, as my parents taught me. Only a *few weeks* ago somebody from the West brought Bibles to our town of Wallachia. Now our family have a lovely new Bible. It is wonderful to be able to read God's Word so easily. Pray for us, please.'

Doug longed to tell the lad the whole story but dared not do so. It was as if God was giving a confirmation of the importance of this work he had given Doug to do. He promised the young Romanian that he would indeed pray for him. That night, at home with his parents, Doug gave thanks to God for the tremendous courage of the Church behind the Iron Curtain. It was so good to be able to share with his parents the joys and sorrows, the encouragements and worries of life. They were interested in everything their son did, without being nosey, or obstructive. Whether it was church involvement, studies in university, leisure pursuits or his football, the Rev. and Mrs. Mackay were interested and did what they could to help.

The days were shortening and the last of the leaves falling from the trees when the draw was announced for the third round of the U.E.F.A. Cup, and the tie awaiting Dalkirk Albion was as uninviting as the weather. They were paired with Dexha F.C., an Albanian team, whose ground was located some eight miles outside the capital, Tirana. The first game was at Brickwell Stadium and gave Albion a chance to build up a strong lead to take to the most closed, isolated society in Europe. Players generally didn't like travelling to Albania, feeling somewhat intimidated by the political atmosphere in the strongly communist state.

As for Doug, he found it strange that once again he might be travelling behind the Iron Curtain, where he could play some small part in serving the beleaguered Church. The days passed, and Mr. Firth made no contact with the youngster, who felt inclined to phone and offer to take Bibles if need be. However, after talking with his father, they agreed that if God wanted him to carry Bibles, he himself would show Doug clearly.

The first-leg match in Dalkirk wasn't an exciting affair. It was generally felt that Dexha had progressed to the third round by dint of defending in depth away from home, and capitalising on the unease of opponents playing in Albania. Dalkirk, on the other hand, were essentially an attacking team with each man playing for his colleagues. This approach proved too much for the visitors who were two goals behind by half time, goals scored by Dawson and Cassidy. As the second half wore on, however, Albion seemed to be running out of ideas to prise open the tight Dexha defence, so with ten minutes to go, Jim Murray committed both his substitutes to the fray in an effort to get the all-important third goal that would make it extremely hard for the Albanians to win over the two matches.

Doug was playing well, without getting into a scoring

position at any point. Then, suddenly, the lad noticed the Dexha keeper preparing to throw the ball out to his left-back, who was out on his own, near the wing. 'Cover him, Taffy,' shouted Doug. Quick as a flash, the Welshman closed down the full back, leaving him only two options, either put the ball out of play for a throw-in, or pass back to the keeper. Doug rightly anticipated he would do the latter, and sprinted into the penalty box in time to intercept the pass-back. Rounding the keeper he made for the byeline and crossed the ball for Fred Thomson to head home.

As the teams trooped off at the end, the faces of the two managers told their own story. Jim Murray was so obviously relieved, but the Dexha manager was disconsolate and grim-faced. He knew now his team's chances of qualifying were very limited. Jim Murray tapped Doug on the shoulder, 'Well done, son! That was quick thinking, we really needed that goal.'

When Doug arrived home, he found his parents looking serious. His father said, 'Mr. Firth phoned this evening to ask if you would consider carrying some Bibles into Albania in a fortnight. He apparently had no intention of asking you to do this because of the risks involved, but he got an appeal from a contact in Eastern Europe. Apparently, there's a small congregation meeting in secret in Albania. They desperately need Bibles and can uplift them in Dexha. This may be their best chance of getting them. It's up to you.'

CHAPTER 6

A DOG'S LIFE

Doug gulped. He had quietly assumed he would be spared this. Now, at almost the last minute, he realised that it was no coincidence Dalkirk Albion had to play yet again behind the Iron Curtain. Lifting the phone he called Mr. Firth.

'Hello, Doug,' began the missionary. Doug sensed there was almost a note of apology in his voice. 'This is a dangerous mission,' Mr. Firth went on. 'If you were to be caught there's no saying what they might do. Personally, I'm not at all sure it's right for you to do this.'

'Aren't the Bibles desperately needed?' asked Doug.

'Yes, they are,' agreed Mr. Firth. 'Apparently, that little congregation have only got one tattered Bible between them and they have to hand round pages of it for reading.'

'We must try,' answered Doug. 'If we were in their position we would want them to try to help us.' Mr. Firth and Doug agreed to meet to discuss the plan they would use to get the Bibles into Dexha.

It was a cold, clear mid-December morning when the Albion players set off for Albania. Dalkirk was getting ready for Christmas, with decorations all along the High Street and the shop windows attractively display-ing a whole range of inviting products. Doug hoped nobody particularly noticed that he was carrying a case rather than a sportsbag. Mr. Firth had reckoned that it was best to conceal the Bibles in a secret compartment about an inch deep right round the inside of the case. Unless the authorities mounted a rigorous search they would not notice the difference between the depth of the inside of the case and the outside.

Their arrival in the Albanian capital introduced them
to a country so different from anything they'd known.
It took their breath away. There was no Christmas
here. Indeed, there seemed to be little festivity or joy of
any kind. The place was dull and, everywhere the team
went, their comparatively pale complexions and rich
clothes attracted suspicious, even sullen, glances. Doug
was feeling nervous as he walked with his team-mates.
At the Customs barrier the officials had insisted on
checking each of the sportsbags belonging to the
Dalkirk squad, together with Doug's case. Each
person's belongings had been emptied out, sifted
through systematically, then replaced, but they had not
noticed anything unusual when they examined the case.
However, the atmosphere in the country was so tense,
Doug felt he might be stopped and searched at any
moment.

'Stop, thief!' It was Simon Barrie shouting. 'Look,
Doug, he's stolen your case!' Doug looked round in
amazement, for it had all happened so quickly. Simon
Barrie was already off in hot pursuit by the time Doug
found his feet and joined the chase. But it was too late:
the case-snatcher dodged into a back street and disappeared.

'What a cheek,' muttered Simon. 'Still he hasn't got
much, though that was a nice case.' Doug wasn't
hearing Simon at all. To his horror he realised that if
the person who had grabbed his case were to rip it open
he would find the Bibles. Since there was little else of
value, he might be tempted to hand the Bibles over to
the police for a reward. The teenager broke out in a
cold sweat. Whatever would he do now! Quietly,
standing there, he prayed that God would keep the
Bibles from falling into the wrong hand, especially
those of the communist authorities.

'Are you all right, chum? You look as if you've just

scored an own goal,' said Simon.

'Ye..s, I'm fine', retorted Doug. 'Let's get back and join the others.'

'We'll get you some other clothes, lad,' said Mr. Delaney, Albion's chairman, who was in charge of the trip. 'Then we can report this matter to the police.'

'OH, NO! Not the police,' Doug blurted out. 'I mean, they could make a real nuisance of themselves to all of us, and put the team off their game tomorrow night. Let's just leave it. We'll soon be out of here.'

'I think the lad's right, Mr. Delaney,' said Sam Barnet. 'The police here aren't like our bobbies back home. They could unsettle us before the game.'

'Fair enough,' said the chairman, reluctantly. 'We'll say nothing for the time being. Let's get back to our coach and check in at the hotel.'

When the team arrived back at the hotel there was yet another surprise waiting for them. Mr. Delaney was handed a large parcel which had arrived only minutes before. On the front, in bold letters, were the words:

'F.C. DALKIRK ALBION'.

'It was left at the door about ten minutes before you arrived,' explained the hotel manager. Mr. Delaney opened the parcel to reveal – Doug's case.

'I can't fathom it out at all,' murmured the chairman. 'What did he steal it for if he wanted to hand it back.' Then, turning to Doug, he said, 'You had better check it, son, to see if anything's missing.'

Doug opened the case quickly and rummaged through the clothes. At once he saw that whoever had taken the case had found the hidden compartments and removed the sixteen Bibles that had been hidden there. The false compartment shelves were gone as well.

'Anything missing?' asked Jim Murray.

'Everything's fine,' replied the teenager.

GOAL BEHIND THE CURTAIN

'A strange carry-on altogether,' said Mr. Delaney.

There was somebody else who was finding it very strange, but he was saying nothing. It was the same member of the Albion squad who had seen visitors to Doug's room in Czechoslovakia and in Romania. 'Hmmm', he thought to himself, 'that's the third time. Mackay's a smuggler. I'm sure of it.'

Alone in his room, Doug was trying to fathom out what had happened. Why would somebody steal his case, then return it? How could they have found the secret compartments so quickly? What could they want with the Bibles anyway? Then all at once it dawned on Doug. Of course, how could he be so slow. The Bibles hadn't been *stolen,* only collected. It must have been a Christian who grabbed the case, and this had been the plan for picking up the precious cargo from the West.

Then Doug shuddered. What might have happened if Simon Barrie had caught up with the Albanian. Everybody would really have been in trouble then: the man, Doug and the whole Dalkirk party. What a relief. Now Doug could relax and try to concentrate on the game next day. With a three-goal lead Albion were favourites to win their way through to a place in the quarter-finals of the competition and, as these games would not take place until March of the following year, there would be a welcome break from the intensity of such high-powered encounters, with all the travelling involved.

No Albanian side had ever qualified for the quarter-finals of a top European Trophy and Dexha were anxious to be the first. The country was politically isolated and saw success in the U.E.F.A. Cup as a means of attracting attention and respect, so there was a real desire to win this game. How real that desire was became clear when Dalkirk ran on to the pitch that evening. The small ground was packed to capacity with about 15,000 fans, who seemed to be so close to the pitch they could almost have been playing on it.

Doug got the impression as he listened to the noise that the football ground would be one of the few places where the people would be free to give vent to their feelings. This opinion was reinforced for the teenager as he watched the police parading round the ground. There must have been about forty of them patrolling the track in pairs, marching stiffly along, heavily armed and looking for all the world as if they were the real centre of attraction with the game as an optional extra.

The thing that caught Doug's attention was that many of them, twenty at least, were in control of savage-looking alsatian dogs. Was this necessary for keeping crowd control, or was it a vain effort to intimidate the Scots? They didn't bother Doug for he had been reared in the Highlands amongst fiercely independent sheep dogs. He was more nervous of the guns. Soon, however, the whistle blew for the kick-off and Doug settled down to concentrate on the game.

Albion had a chance to tie the game up in the first minute, a bad pass-back from a Dexha defender putting Fred Thomson clean through. Fred steadied himself and shot low to the keeper's right hand, and then raised his hands in the air as he saw the ball slip under the man's diving body. But his delight was short-lived as the ball hit the inside of the post and rolled agonisingly along the goal line to strike the other post before being cleared by a defender. Gradually, Dexha, spurred on by their noisy fans, gained control of the game and Loslehi, their star striker who had missed the first game through injury, opened the scoring.

In the second half, Dexha began where they had left off and Loslehi, in particular, was causing all sorts of problems for Albion's defence. In the twenty-third minute of the second half he robbed Tom Pearson and charged into the penalty-box. Doug, chasing hard after him slid in and though he didn't disposess the big striker, he did enough to unsettle him with the result that his strong drive went past Simon Barrie's left hand post – much to the extreme annoyance of an unfortunate alsatian which got the full impact of it and was knocked off its feet. The dog barked angrily throughout the rest of the match.

With only ten minutes to go, however, Loslehi gave the Albanian crowd something to shout about. Picking up a long ball out of defence he beat three Albion defenders before firing a magnificent twenty-yard shot into the roof of the net. From now till the final whistle Albion would have to hold on by their fingertips. Jim Murray had been right. Dalkirk had really needed that third goal, made by Doug in their home leg. But would it be enough? Loslehi was on the run again, leaving a trail of stranded defenders behind him. Doug had never seen such a player. No wonder the Albanians were doing so well in the competition.

Now there was only Simon Barrie between the striker and his target. The crowd was screaming with anticipation. Suddenly there was a flurry of activity on the track behind the goal. Loslehi hammered the ball and Barrie was beaten. But the ball never reached the net. Instead a yelp of pain indicated that the unfortunate Albanian striker had landed another one on the even more unfortunate alsatian. The animal, frantic with excitement had seen its tormentor and rushed straight at him, only to be hit again, but though the dog couldn't know it, it had delivered a far greater blow to the Dexha striker than he had given it.

The crowd were furious and roared their disapproval in the direction of the embarrassed policeman who had been taken by surprise by the sudden, powerful lunge of the dog that had pulled the lead right out of his hands. The Dexha supporters were further incensed by the referee's decision – a bounce-up three yards from goal. It was, of course, the only fair decision in the circumstances, and referee Rolf, from West Germany, was brave enough to give it.

The danger, however, was not yet over. A bounce-up three yards from goal with Loslehi on the end of it, was a frightening prospect. Tom Pearson went in for the bounce-up from Albion's side. He'd had a nightmare of a game. Normally so safe, he simply hadn't contained the big Dexha striker at all. The referee dropped the ball. Once again, Tom was beaten as Loslehi swiped at the ball. He connected, but the ball cannoned off Tom Pearson and out for a corner, which was cleared.

Albion held out for the few minutes that remained and left the field three-two winners on aggregate over the two games. The frustration of the fans boiled over and extra police had to be drafted in before they would disperse. 'Wonder what will happen to that dog?' asked Doug, with concern in his voice.

'The Boss should sign it up as a reserve for Simon,' cracked Norrie Harvey. 'That really was an amazing save.'

The Dalkirk players were shattered, the tension had really got to them, with the result that few of them had played up to their normal standard. In addition, the Albanian team had been good, far better than earlier reports had suggested. All things considered, Jim Murray was happy as he went round the dressing-room congratulating the players.

'We're through to the quarter-finals, and that's the main thing. It's a great performance for a wee club.'

'Let's hope we get one of the glamour clubs in the quarter-finals. That would be a real treat for the Dalkirk fans,' said Mr. Delaney.

GOAL BEHIND THE CURTAIN

'Let's hope we get home first,' growled Norrie Harvey, as the door opened to reveal a large, rather grim policeman.

'Doug Mackay, pleeze,' he said in gruff English, 'out here.' Doug gulped. How had they found out? Had the Christians been arrested and forced to talk? As he came out of the dressing-room the policeman led him to a room at the back of the grandstand and ushered him in. There were only two persons in the room, a photographer and the Dexha striker, Loslehi, whose skills had so impressed the teenager. The Albanian held out his hand, 'Well played. It waz your goal in Scotland that beat uz. You worked for that goal. You earned it.' Pointing to the camera he added, 'We have a picture.'

Doug sighed with relief. He had feared the worst, but all was well, and he was really honoured to have his photograph taken with this outstanding player. 'I wish you were playing in our League at home. It would be great for football – if you were playing for Dalkirk Albion.' The big fellow smiled, shook hands and said goodbye.

As Doug walked back to his dressing-room, he wondered if he would ever see the man again. He longed to speak more to him about football, but even more he found inside himself a deep yearning to share the gospel of Christ with the man – to tell him *God loved the whole world so much he gave his only Son to save us all from sin.* He prayed that God would use him to win other people for Christ. He was becoming increasingly convinced nothing else mattered as much as this.

It was great to be back home again, Doug had so much to talk over with his parents. He found that as a result of his European experience and the demands they were making on his faith, he wanted to talk, and more particularly, to listen to his father. He needed to

A DOG'S LIFE

know God better, to hear more about him. He saw
young Christians who were living rather selfishly, not
really putting their faith into practice, but once you
took the claims of Christ seriously, you needed the
wisdom and encouragement of older Christian friends
and family.

At Christmas, young people from the church went
out singing carols. Doug joined them and was asked to
speak for a few minutes between songs. They were
outside a busy supermarket with shoppers hurrying to
and fro. As the youngster spoke, a crowd began to
gather, made up mainly of young lads who saw Doug
regularly at Brickwell Stadium. They listened intently
as he spoke for they saw him as one of themselves.

Soon such a crowd was gathering that it was obvious
there would be serious inconvenience to shoppers using
the supermarket, so Doug concluded by urging the
people to attend a Christmas Eve service of which there
would be plenty in the area.

When he got home that day he learned that Albion
had got the plum draw of the U.E.F.A. Cup quarter-
finals: they were to play Morino of Italy, the favourites,
with no less than seven members of the Italian international side, including the brilliant Guiseppe Sabelli,
reckoned the best midfield player in the world.

CHAPTER 7

HALF-TIME

Unlike most colleges in the country, Stirling University favoured the American Semester system, which meant that courses were divided into two parts with a month-long break around February. Doug had fully intended staying at home and relaxing, as far as he could relax with all the commitments he had in church and on the football field. During the month of January, however, something happened which set his thoughts moving in a different direction altogether.

The snow had been falling steadily all day, and by evening the lovely University campus was covered with a wintry white blanket. Doug and some friends were attending a Christian Union meeting that evening and finding the warm friendship of the gathering a welcome change from the near Arctic conditions outside. The meeting was an informal one and the speaker was a representative of a missionary society working in Brazil. It was a fascinating country and the keen, lively Christianity of many in the land was heartening to see.

As he drew his talk to a close the speaker appealed for students to consider going to Brazil for their month-long holiday. They would be expected to find their own fare, but once in the country the mission would take care of them and set them to work. Doug was very interested, not just because he liked to travel, but because he realised such an experience as this could help him see more clearly what his life's work might be.

He prayed on his way home that night and sensed the rightness of such a trip. This was confirmed for him by his Bible-reading for the evening, for he had been reading in the Book of Acts in the New Testament and had

56

come to chapter 8. As he read verses 25 to 40 of the chapter, he felt he could identify with one of the people described there, Philip, a deacon in the early church.

The man had been busily involved in the work of the Lord when he heard the call to leave what he was doing. 'Rise and go toward the south,' he was told. The command would have taken Philip by surprise, but he obeyed because he trusted God. What followed for Philip was the wonderful privilege of leading a man to put his faith in Christ. That man had gone back to his home in Africa to introduce the gospel to that great continent, where, as Doug realised, there were now millions of Christians.

'What a good thing Philip did what God wanted,' thought Doug. 'I must be prepared to go to Brazil if that's what the Lord wants.'

There were a few practical problems, however, not the least of which was the cost of the fare to Rio. A telephone call to a travel agent revealed that the price of a return ticket was £830 – and that was with a good reduction for students – a concessionary ticket, as it was called. Doug did not have that kind of money. Then there was football. He was getting his game every week and fulfilling all his early promise. Dalkirk Albion were in a healthy position in the Premier Division table and Jim Murray wouldn't want the squad disturbed for a month.

Not least there was church. Doug was involved with young people's work, through Bible Class, Youth Fellowship and Boy's Brigade. Also he was a member of the Squad – a group of men and lads who attended to the many practical tasks around the church, such as repairs, tidying etc. Doug enjoyed the Squad. Not only was it good for laughs, giving him the opportunity to indulge his mischievous sense of humour, but it was a place where he learned many valuable lessons. Some of these lessons were practical, others were spiritual. Doug loved to hear the men recount their stories of how God had helped them and increased their faith. Their experiences were sometimes funny, often serious, but always helpful, and Doug's own faith blossomed in the healthy, happy atmosphere of working fellowship.

One thing Doug noticed about the Squad was that no member ever spoke critically of any of the others. They could be trusted with each others' reputations. He knew these men were his friends.

Thinking of all these commitments made Doug feel he couldn't possibly go to Brazil. Then he looked again at the story of Philip the deacon. He, too, had been a busy man doing an important work, yet he was called for a time to go somewhere else. Doug could only think of one answer to this problem, an answer often tried and never found to fail. Bowing his head, he prayed, 'Lord, if you want me to go to Brazil, please provide the money and give me time off from the league programme? And, Lord, please provide someone else to help in my place in the church?'

Having prayed, Doug was able to go to bed with a sense of peace filling his heart. Next day the teenager attended Brickwell Stadium for training. As usual, it had been a tough session and he was making his way from the pitch to the dressing-room, when manager Jim Murray caught up with him. 'Could you come to my office for a moment, Doug?' he said.

Once in the office the lad noticed something unusual. The manager looked a little uncomfortable, not at all his usual unruffled self.

'Tell you what it is, boy,' he blurted out. 'I want you to take a break for a few weeks.'

Doug's eyes widened, as the manager, Jim Murray, hastened to explain. 'We have an important spell starting in March, with the U.E.F.A. Cup and the run in for the Premier League. We may still be in the Scottish Cup by that time and we'll need all the fresh legs we can get. It's going to be tough for all the players, but for you it's going to be worse than any, not just because you are the youngest, but because you play an all-action game, hardly stopping. If you go on through the next month like that you'll be snookered when we need you most.'

'Great!' cried Doug excitedly. Then he explained to Jim Murray about the possible trip to Brazil, being careful to miss out the point about not having the fare. The manager beamed with delight. He was relieved Doug had taken the news so well. He didn't want to tell him that he was resting him because the teenager was vitally important to his plans for the rest of the season. Doug could have a great future in football – if that was where his future lay.

'There's another thing,' said Jim Murray, drawing an envelope from his pocket. 'The Directors asked me to pass this on to you. It's a gift from the Board. We can't pay you as an amateur, but we are allowed to give you a small gift. It should come in handy for Brazil.'

Doug thanked the manager and, making a mental note to write a letter of gratitude to the Board of Directors, he got changed and went home. Once home, he discovered to his delight, that the envelope contained £1,000 which would not only cover his return student fare to Rio, but also enable him to give a gift to the work of mission behind the Iron Curtain. Doug thanked God for another prayer answered.

At tea, Alec Mackay announced that he was to have an assistant for two months, starting that very weekend. The young man in question had been attached to a number of congregations in the area, rather than to one congregation as was the more normal practice. The idea behind this arrangement was that, in the course of his year's assistantship, the prospective minister would get as wide an experience as possible of the various kinds of parishes.

'I was thinking, Doug, he could take on some of your duties for a spell,' said his father. It was fantastic. In less than twenty-four hours Doug had seen three obstacles to his Brazilian trip disappear as if they had never been there at all. As he told his parents they shared his excitement and the conviction that this trip was not only right but important.

The day of the flight dawned clear and cold. As he boarded the flight, Doug recalled the trips he'd made in those recent months: Czechoslovakia, Romania, Albania and now Brazil. The verse from St. Paul's letter to one of the early churches sprang to mind – 'being penniless, yet possessing all things'. Truly, this was it. The world was his oyster, yet he was learning to live not for the world, but for God, who in his love for men and women everywhere, gave his Son, Jesus, to be their Saviour.

Doug found Brazil to be a beautiful country. The lochs and mountains of his boyhood home had bred in him a love for beauty wherever he found it. Yet, though the countryside was beautiful and the upperclass areas of the city were impressive, there was another side. Doug was saddened to see some of the poverty and even squalor that existed. The mission he was with for the month placed him in a large city many miles from Rio. There were four fellows and six girls in the team and they were to be living in five different homes with members of the congregation to which they were attached.

Doug shared a room with Claude, a French student, who spoke excellent English. Their room was very simple. There was no floor covering on the bare boards and only a flimsy curtain on the single window. There was a rather tired-looking wardrobe with a single drawer at the bottom to accommodate the clothes of both lads, and there were two old chairs. There were two camp beds supplied by the mission and a rickety table at which the boys could study or write letters. In one corner of the room was an old-fashioned sink with only one tap. There was no hot water, just as there was no heating of any kind in the room.

Although conditions seemed spartan to Doug he soon discovered they were superior to those of many working people in Brazil, some of whom had no running water and no inside toilet. Doug and Claude even had an electric socket on one wall of their room so that they could listen to a cassette player. Furthermore, the absence of heating was not a serious problem as the weather didn't turn really cold in that area.

The work in which Doug and his friends were involved was mainly that of sharing the Good News of Jesus Christ with the people, who were very open-hearted and friendly, willing to listen to the students and speak frankly about their spiritual needs.

Doug quickly felt a deep attachment to them and was really glad that he was able to help different ones in practical ways, because of his experience with the Squad in the church back home. He could mend a leaking roof here and repair a television set there; it was good to be able to help where so much was needed. Doug saw that one of the major problems facing the people was the cost of living, due to the high rate of inflation. It was so bad that one Japanese company was advertising television sets with a promise that your money would be refunded in two years' time. That sounded wonderful until you realised that with an inflation rate of over 1000% the money that purchased a TV set today would hardly buy a torch battery in two years' time.

Such poverty was deeply upsetting to the youngster and he felt within him a growing desire to spend his life sharing the gospel with the poor and helping them in whatever way he could. How he appreciated the privileges he had back home in Britain and which he had taken for granted up until that time.

It wasn't all one way, however, Doug was receiving as well as giving. When Sunday arrived, for example, he was impressed to see how many people attended church. There were hundreds of men, women and children crowding into buildings of all shapes and sizes. The worship was lively and the people seemed to pay close attention to the whole service.

On the football field also Doug was learning new things. There was the confidence of the players to express their skills, a confidence that seemed to run through the whole of Brazilian life. The game flowed easily, and there wasn't the fear of making mistakes that crippled the British game. Then there was the "bicycle kick" as it was called, a trick Doug had never seen before. It involved flicking the ball up in the air with one foot and shooting with the other, before either foot had touched the ground again. It was a gravity-defying trick, and one Doug made up his mind to master.

All too soon the month was over and it was time to return home. The warmth and kindness of the Brazilian people had made a huge impression on the students, and there were tearful farewells all round. As the plane rose high above Rio, Doug wondered if he would ever return to this sad and lovely land which had wound its way around his heart so quickly. Only slowly did his mind return to home and the tasks awaiting him. Increasingly, the question came to his mind: What of Morino? How will we cope with them, the pride of

HALF-TIME

Italy, the giants of Europe. The young Scot would find
out soon enough.

CHAPTER 8

MAN OF A MILLION POUNDS

Dalkirk Albion had not done particularly well during the month of February. They had been knocked out of the Scottish Cup and lost two important league matches. The sheer pressure of competing with full-time outfits on heavy, stamina-sapping pitches had taken its inevitable toll. Many of the players were looking jaded and discouraged when Doug breezed in for his first training session, sporting a light sun tan.

'Huh! These feather-bedded students,' grumbled Simon Barrie darkly. 'It's easy for them, sunbathing all day on beaches.'

'Actually, we spent most of the time hunting for rats,' announced Doug mischievously. There was a stunned silence, broken by his added comment, 'Well, we had to have *something* to eat.' This was received with a chorus of good-humoured jeering and a well-aimed shinguard which hit Doug on the back of the head.

Jim Murray grinned. He was glad to have his youngest player back. His positive attitude was good for morale and the other players respected his ability. Maybe he could help lift them that little bit more.

The training session over, the team for the first leg in Italy was announced and Doug was glad to see he was included in the starting line-up. The time in Brazil had whetted his appetite for the game and he could hardly wait to get started.

Canario Stadium, home ground of Morino, was most impressive. It could take 120,000 fans, all seated, and provided the most comfortable facilities for the players and staff. The Italians had given the Albion party a friendly enough reception, but they were barely able to disguise their contempt for the part-timers from the little Lowland town. Albion's recent defeats in domestic competitions had encouraged the belief that they had lost form and would offer little resistance to the Roman conquerors.

There was a capacity crowd as the two teams walked on to the pitch, and the atmosphere was something the Scots had never experienced before. Having lost the toss they kicked off and were immediately under pressure thanks to a succession of nervously misplaced passes which handed possession over to the home side. Morino were determined to finish the game off in the first half.

Doug couldn't believe how completely his team-mates had lost confidence and it was no surprise when they went behind in eight minutes to a skilfully-worked goal. Guiseppe Sabelli, their million pound midfield genius, dispossessed Rob Malloy and drew Tom Pearson out of position before sliding a perfect pass through for Caponi, the striker, to score.

The Albion players began to grumble at each other, a thing Doug had never seen them do before. Simon Barrie was exceptionally vocal. He sounded very bitter. Worse was to follow for three minutes later Sabelli threaded his way through the Dalkirk rear guard and only a last second tackle by Doug foiled him in the very act of shooting. From the resulting corner Caponi rose above the defence to head a great goal. The Albion players were devastated. Their heads went down and Simon Barrie raged as the crowd began to chant something that sounded rather like 'EASY, EASY'.

Doug had never seen anything like it. If this continued they would be ashamed to go home again. What would the Brazilians do? The thought flashed through the teenager's mind. They wouldn't put up with this nonsense, he thought. 'Come on, boys,' he shouted, 'it's only 2–0. We can still beat them.' But nobody was listening. Doug remembered what his father had once said in a different context: 'When people won't *listen* to you, at least sometimes they'll *look* at you, and you can win them that way'.

That was it. Doug would start a one-man fight-back, and maybe that would lift these reluctant heroes. Sabelli collected a pass and strode forward purposefully, arrogance written all over his swarthy features. Doug chased him and robbed him easily, for he simply wasn't expecting any resistance. The lad linked up with Norrie Harvey and ran forward for the return pass. Harvey's pass was atrocious and gave Morino possession again. The midfielder Rivera strolled up the wing with the ball only to find himself the subject of a hefty tackle from Doug, who passed again to Norrie Harvey. This time the left-back picked out Fred Thomson with a great 40-yard pass. The striker, however, missed his kick and the ball was back with Sabelli. Looking up the play-maker aimed a pass to the left-wing, but he kicked fresh air, for the ball was nipped off his feet by Doug who was here, there and everywhere like a blue and gold pimpernel.

The teenager set off on a mazy dribble that took him past three Morino defenders. He slipped a neat pass to Fred Thomson who picked out Bill Dawson with a lovely back-heel. The big striker out-paced the defender who was marking him and fired in a tremendous shot, which was net-bound all the way until Alcomo in Morino's goal rose to tip it over the bar. It was a piece of remarkable goal-keeping that brought the huge crowd to its feet.

Dalkirk were growing in confidence, while the Italians were becoming increasingly rattled. Doug's will to win was getting through to his team-mates. Now, all of them were harrying and chasing their opponents, giving them no time to settle on the ball, while keeping possession to themselves as long as possible whenever they won the ball. But to lose a goal just before half-time could be a bad blow psychologically. Sabelli set off on a determined run which left two Albion defenders stranded. Doug went to meet him, but the star neatly shoved the ball through his legs and ran round him, to beat another opponent. But Doug was blocking his path again. The Italian swerved past the youngster and made for the penalty-box, where he side-stepped the only defender left between him and the goal – only to find Doug was back in position to tackle him again. The irritation showed in Sabelli's face. He was clever, but even he was running out of tricks. Then he saw his chance, for the young Scot was moving to his left as if anticipating the Italian to go that way. Sabelli swung the opposite way – just as Doug had planned. Quick as a flash he slid into the tackle and knocked the ball away.

Sabelli was livid. He swung his boot at Doug and hit him on the thigh. It was a bad foul, utterly unworthy of a player of that calibre, and if Doug had rolled around in mock agony, 'making a meal of it', the Norwegian referee would have had no alternative but to send Sabelli off. Instead the lad got to his feet and extended his right hand to the Italian. His handshake was refused. Sabelli was cautioned and shown the yellow card.

In Albion's dressing-room, spirits were high, as Jim Murray and Sam Barnet encouraged their team to keep fighting back and to try for that all important away goal. However, the second half produced no further scoring, although there were thrills aplenty as Albion fought a brave defensive battle against an extremely skilful side.

The game was marred in the closing minutes when the surly Sabelli was finally ordered off for protesting too vehemently against a decision by the referee, who had been very fair and had kept a sound grip of the match. Now the Italians would have to face the second leg in Scotland without their star player. Somehow there seemed to be a little less self-confidence in the Morino camp at the end of the game than there had been at the beginning.

The performance in Rome really raised Albion's morale and they went on to win their next two league matches, before the visit of Morino.

The Dalkirk Board of Directors had been tempted to move the fixture to a larger ground which could have accommodated three times the crowd Brickwell Stadium could hold. This would have brought in much more money for the club, enabling them to buy players who would strengthen their pool. In the end, however, they had decided to sacrifice financial gain and keep faith with their loyal supporters, a gesture that was greatly appreciated by the fans.

All 20,000 tickets for the match had been sold more than a week in advance and the ground was packed when the teams took the field. The visitors had not endeared themselves to the Albion directors by their disparaging references to Brickwell Stadium as a 'training pitch', and their players made themselves even less popular with the crowd in the opening minutes as they gave away a succession of free kicks for rash tackles. It quickly became obvious that Doug was the chief target of Morino's rough stuff and the Portuguese referee had to wave the yellow card above the heads of two Italians before they got the message. As the first half progressed Taffy Rosser, on the right wing, was proving to be Albion's danger man and it was fitting that he should open the scoring with a high cross-cum-shot which eluded the keeper, and slipped in at the far post.

MAN OF A MILLION POUNDS

Morino were clearly missing the skills of Sabelli, and the second half was only six minutes old when hesitancy in their defence cost them another goal. Doug started the move, beating his man and sending a defence-splitting pass to Eric Cassidy on the left wing. He cut inside, drew two defenders with him and gave Rob Malloy the easiest of shooting chances to tie the scores up at 2-2 on aggregate. The Brickwell crowd were going frantic at the prospect of yet another outstanding European victory. After all, if Albion could beat Morino they could go all the way and become the first Scottish side to win the Trophy.

Raid after raid was mounted on the visitors' goal, most of them orchestrated by Doug or Ron Macleod, who were calming the play down and dominating the midfield exchanges. Things began to look grim for the continental side as first Cassidy, then Pearson, went close with tremendous drives which brought the best out of goalkeeper Alcomo. The visitors' confidence slowly began to return, however, as the game drew to a close, with the prospect of extra time looming up. As full-time professionals they would have a tremendous advantage over the leg-weary Albion players, most of whom had completed a normal day's work before stepping on to the field that evening. Time was running out for the home side, as Norrie Harvey passed the ball to Doug deep inside the Dalkirk half of the field. Caponi lunged at the youngster, hoping to win the ball and bear down on goal. Doug clipped the ball smartly off one foot on to the other and sped past the big striker. Moving rapidly Doug advanced to the half-way line where two Morino players challenged him. Hearing Norrie Harvey calling for the ball, Doug shoved it between the two defenders and ran to the left wing as Norrie penetrated the visitors' half.

Sensing the danger, Vanete, the sweeper, came out

to meet Harvey who chipped the ball over his head for Doug to chase. There were two defenders on his tail as the youngster powered his way into the penalty-box amidst the frenzied roar of the crowd. Alcomo charged out to tackle him, but Doug veered left, pushing the ball towards the bye-line. He just managed to reach it before it went over and swung a cross toward the goal. Three defenders rose for the ball with Norrie Harvey in the goal-mouth, but the big Englishman out-jumped them all to head the winner.

Amidst the incredible scenes of celebration that followed, hardly anyone noticed a crumpled figure lying beside the byeline. Doug hadn't seen the goal, for he had been poleaxed by a crude tackle, and as he lay there he sensed this was a bad injury. At last the stretcher was brought on and he was carried to the pavilion. The injury to his left leg was more painful than anything he'd ever known, yet he felt so glad Albion had made it.

What should have been the happiest moment of Jim Murray's managerial career was given over to concern as he saw the youngster's pain-torn features.

'That was an appalling tackle,' he said angrily. 'More like an assault.'

'We're through anyway. That's the main thing,' said Doug, playing it down. 'This injury may heal quickly.'

Jim Murray said nothing. He knew a nasty injury when he saw one. This could be a fracture, in which case Doug would be out for the rest of the season.

An examination in hospital revealed a badly-bruised shin, and while it would not be necessary for Doug to have treatment, he certainly would require a long spell of rest before returning to training again, let alone taking part in a match. It looked as if he wouldn't be turning in any more dazzling performances in the U.E.F.A. Cup that season.

MAN OF A MILLION POUNDS

A few days after the Morino match Doug was resting at home and studying maths when he heard the door-bell. He recognised the voice at once as belonging to Jim Murray who had called to see him. They chatted for a while mostly about Doug's injury and then the manager announced with a smile, 'I've got some good news for you. There's been a transfer bid made for you.'

Doug looked genuinely surprised. 'But I'm a student,' he answered. 'I want to finish my course. Besides, I'm not sure football is meant to be my career.'

'Well, I daresay this club can find a way round your problems.'

'Which club is it?' asked Doug.

'Morino,' replied Jim Murray.

Doug looked astonished, hardly able to take the idea in. 'They offered £1,000,000 for you. That was after the *first* match in Rome. After the *second* leg they doubled the offer.'

'£2,000,000,' gasped Doug.

'Yes, and a direct payment of £200,000 to yourself before you even kick a ball for them,' added the manager quietly. 'It's a tremendous offer; the chance of a lifetime.'

Doug was silent for a moment before he replied. 'It's too big a decision for me to make. I'll have to pray about it, and then talk it over with my Dad.'

Jim Murray listened enviously. Here was someone less than half his age, yet who knew how to face every kind of decision and problem in life, great or small, with confidence that the right answer would always be given as long as there was the readiness to do God's will. Being willing! That was the problem for Albion's boss. Like most men he found it hard to vacate the driving seat of his life and hand the keys over to God. But was he right? The more he got to know young

Mackay the less sure he felt of himself.

A badly-bruised leg gives a busy Christian time to grumble – or to pray. Doug plumped for the latter, relieved that he could spend many of the hours of forced inactivity, not only swotting for exams, but reading his Bible and talking to his heavenly Father. At first the lad saw it as a simple, straight-forward choice – for or against moving to Morino and, frankly he hoped the answer was No; to him football was *sport*. To the men at the high cash end of the scale it was a soul-less business, pure and simple, motivated by an unquenchable thirst for money and fame, and marked by cynical fouls and shameful aggression. Wasn't that the very reason he himself was a temporary invalid? But the more he thought about it the more he realised his decision was not for or against Morino as a team, but for or against football as a career.

To pursue football as a career one must go all the way, for the player's life is a short one and full of uncertainty – a manager's life even more so. A lad of nineteen could not afford to scorn such an offer as this and expect the opportunity to arise again. Doug could say 'No' to Morino and go on enjoying his football, but he could not expect the high priests of football to forgive him for his choice which dared to suggest there could be a greater God than 'The Game'. As Doug read in the letter of James, chapter 1:17, the words confirmed for him the decision already forming in his mind: *'every good and every perfect gift comes down from above from the Father of lights with whom there is no variation or shadow due to change.'*

Yes, football is a great gift, thought Doug, but the Giver is more important than the gifts. I cannot become a soccer slave, my best years bought and paid for me by men. I must be free to serve God

MAN OF A MILLION POUNDS

as he leads me.

CHAPTER 9

FIGHT TO THE FINISH

The staff and players of Dalkirk Albion were happy to see Doug on his return to Brickwell Stadium after the leg injury. They had been really good to the lad sending him cards, flowers and fruit, and making occasional visits to his home. The training session was hard and punishing, as Jim Murray strove to get his men ready for their forthcoming U.E.F.A. Cup semi-final with Abranov of Moscow. Such opposition would be well drilled and the Albion players would need all the pace and stamina they could get. Doug looked on wistfully, longing to be out there with them and he prayed that the healing of his leg might be speeded up, for he hadn't given up hope of being able to play again by the end of the season. Jim Murray put Sam Barnet in charge for the last half-hour of the session and trotted over to see Doug.

'I was hoping to get a chat with you, Mr Murray,' said the boy. 'I've come to a decision on the Morino question.'

'Fine, Doug,' replied the boss, 'I'll see you in my office in fifteen minutes, just as soon as I've had a shower and changed.'

Doug sensed the man was slightly tense as he hurried off and that impression was reinforced quarter of an hour later as they sat down to talk in the manager's office. The youngster carefully explained his thoughts and feelings about the matter and he was relieved to see how Jim Murray respected his decision. The boss even managed a smile as he pictured the look of unbelief on the face of Morino manager Pibuelo when he heard of Doug's decision.

The manager put his hand on Doug's shoulder,

'Thanks very much, what you've said has been a great help to me and I know it will be a real encouragement to the boys.' Then, as Doug left the office, Jim Murray added, 'I'd like you to be there when I break the news to the boys. I know you don't like being the centre of attraction, but I think you should hear what I have to say.'

Once in the dressing-room, Jim Murray called for attention and explained Doug's decision to his team-mates. It was received with raised eyebrows and gasps of astonishment.

'Do you think they'll take me instead, boss?' asked Norrie Harvey with a grin.

Jim Murray ignored the crack. 'There's something else,' he said. 'Morino have also approached me to become their manager. I too will be saying NO. There are more important things in life than financial success.'

The players were stunned, but as the reality of what they had heard dawned upon them they realised there was something very special about belonging to this modest little football club. What it was they weren't quite sure yet, but it made them want to play Abranov off the park.

It was just as well the Albion players were fired with high ideals and loyal team spirit as they faced Abranov, for the Russians were even better than the Scots had expected. They certainly hadn't come to Brickwell Stadium to defend, or to strangle the game in midfield. Instead, they pressed forward at every opportunity and deservedly led by one goal to nil at half time. Albion did pull a goal back early in the second half, but in their desperation to grab a winner they left themselves exposed at the back once too often and the team from Moscow scored. Thanks to their superior fitness they were able to hold on to their lead to the final whistle.

GOAL BEHIND THE CURTAIN

It was a devastating blow to Dalkirk. Although their fans cheered them off the field no one was in any doubt about the size of the task that faced the club now. To lose *one* goal at home was bad enough, but to lose two – *and* lose the home leg itself. Usually, there was no way back from such a reverse. However, Jim Murray was not the sort of man to give up in a crisis. He encouraged the players and coaxed that little bit extra out of them in training. Slowly, but surely, he persuaded them that the tie was far from over.

The manager stuck to his task bravely and wisely. None of the players had any idea of the conflict raging within him. Then one evening the telephone rang in Alec Mackay's manse. It was Jim Murray and he wanted to talk about the gospel. That night the manager called to see Doug's father and they talked for hours in the study. When they finally emerged Jim Murray looked a more relaxed man and he couldn't wait to tell Doug the good news.

'I've known there was something missing from my life for a long time, but I could never work out what. I kept thinking of religion as a duty I had to perform to please a God I could never know. That was until I met you and realised that you *knew* God as a person. You were living for someone you knew and cared about, because you knew he cared about you. When you turned down the chance to go to Morino, it was an act of wholehearted obedience to a God you knew. But when I said 'No' to Morino it was different. With me it was a cry for help. I wanted to know God as you know him, and tonight, thanks to your father's help, I believe I have taken that first all-important step of faith.'

Doug was thrilled to hear Jim Murray speak like this. It not only confirmed that his own decision not to join Morino had been correct, but it showed him how important his example was in influencing other people.

People were watching him as a Christian, not to find fault, but to strengthen their own struggling faith.

As the days passed, Doug found something else that gave him pleasure. His bruised leg was healing more quickly than had been expected. He was able to resume light training before the team was selected for the second leg U.E.F.A. Cup match in Moscow and, to his great delight, he was chosen to travel with the squad for the match. He had received work home from University and was well up to date, having used his spell of enforced rest wisely.

That very evening Doug received a telephone call from Mr. Firth. The missionary sounded excited. He had been watching the sports programme on television and had heard the news of Doug's selection.

'We have recently had a request from a large unregistered congregation in Moscow,' Mr. Firth began. 'They are anxious to get some Bibles from us. Do you think you could help again – you and Hesperus?'

The teenager was quiet for a moment. It hadn't really registered with him that he was going behind the Iron Curtain once more, with another great opportunity to help his fellow-Christians. 'Why, ye..es, certainly, Mr. Firth. I'm ready – and so is Hesperus. But we leave Dalkirk on Monday morning. There isn't much time.'

'No problem, lad. I'll bring the Bibles round at eight o'clock on Monday morning. We'll leave the pick-up procedure to the Russians. Thanks again, Doug. We all really appreciate this more than we can tell you.'

That Sunday, in church, Doug paid particular attention to his father's sermon, for he was preaching about Paul's words to the church in Corinth: *'In weakness God's strength is made perfect'*.

The sermon did help Doug who felt very weak. He

hadn't played a match since his injury against Morino. How would he manage to cope if he was sent on against Abranov? Then there were the Bibles. This time he was smuggling them into the main country behind the Iron Curtain, Moscow, the nerve-centre of communism. The risk he was taking sent a shiver up his spine. But the Lord was with him and he would protect him through it all.

As he boarded the plane taking the team to Moscow he reflected on the words his Mum had shared with him from her Bible-reading that morning. They were from Hebrews, chapter 13, verse 6: *'The Lord is my helper, I will not be afraid; what can man do to me?'*

At first Doug felt tense, but gradually as he thought of those words he became more relaxed, and was able to chat more with Eric Cassidy who was sitting next to him on the flight. The young Irishman was playing from the start of the match and nerves had been getting the better of him. Doug's chatter helped him feel more at ease. He was a good player with an excellent future in the game and already Dalkirk Albion were getting the benefits of his skills. As the plane approached Moscow Airport for touchdown, Doug felt a growing uneasiness that he could not explain. His attention was taken by a little girl dressed in a nurse's uniform, and gradually he found a plan forming in his mind.

'Excuse me,' Doug asked one of the air hostesses, 'could we have the teddy-bear from the luggage compartment when we land, there will probably be photographers when we get there and Hesperus likes to be in the picture.'

The air hostess smiled: 'I'm sure he's not a security threat.'

Doug's lips felt dry as he smiled back. The words "Security Threat" made him feel more than a little uneasy.

FIGHT TO THE FINISH

As the passengers waited to disembark, Hesperus was carried through by the air hostess. 'Here he is,' she gasped. 'And if you ask me he needs to be put on a diet.'

'He's always the same when he flies,' grinned Doug. 'It's all the rich food you give us.' He hoped the hostess hadn't seen how nervous he was, but she was already turning round to speak to another passenger.

'Look at the bear, look at the bear!' cried the little girl in the nurse's uniform. Just as Doug had hoped, Hesperus was attracting attention from the right quarter.

'How would you like your photograph taken with this celebrity?' asked Doug, smiling to the little girl's parents.

'He's not a seppity, he's a bear,' Nursey answered, reaching out to cuddle Hesperus.

'He's not feeling very well,' said Doug solemnly. 'You wouldn't have a bandage in your nurse's case by any chance?'

'Yes, I have,' she answered smartly, pulling out a piece of crêpe that was just big enough to go round Hesperus' large head.

Airport officials and photographers alike were amazed to see Dalkirk Albion staff and players emerge from the plane led by a diminutive nurse holding the arm of a teddy-bear which was being carried horizontally by two football players, bedecked in blue and gold scarves and bonnets. Hesperus not only had a bandage on his head, but the little nurse's cap on his tummy. The press loved it and the Customs officials hardly gave the pantomime a second look as they turned, grim-faced, to the serious business of looking for smugglers.

It took the Albion staff longer than usual to clear Customs. The Russians were making no exceptions and every item of luggage was searched. Almost certainly Hesperus would have faced the same check but for Doug's quick thinking. When their coach arrived at the hotel the weary players and officials were escorted to their rooms, but as they were making their way inside they heard an angry shout. Turning round Doug saw the irate bus driver waving his fist at someone who had jumped into his seat and was driving the bus away.

'Hoi, our luggage is still on board,' shouted Jim Murray, setting off in hot pursuit.

'Too late, boss!' called Bill Dawson. 'You won't catch him now.'

'That's our kit gone,' moaned Mr. Delaney. 'If they'd been half as interested in it here as they were at the airport, it would still be here,' he added bitterly.

Within minutes the police arrived and set off in the general direction of the vanishing bus. Doug noticed Jim Murray had calmed down. He was concerned, no doubt of that, but he was trusting God to have a purpose even in this.

The police soon returned to announce triumphantly that they had found the bus. It had been abandoned less than a mile away and the luggage appeared to be still intact, locked in the boot. Even as he listened, Doug guessed what had happened.

'Where's the bear?' It was Eric Cassidy who asked the question. He had become quite attached to Hesperus.

'Imagine going to these lengths to steal a teddy-bear,' said Les Fernie. 'You would think it was filled with gold.'

Some of the others laughed at the comment, but one member of the party raised his eyebrows. So that's it, he thought. That's how it's done. Ah well, smarty Mackay, we'll see what the KGB think of *that* before we leave Russia.

FIGHT TO THE FINISH

It was a cool April evening as the two teams walked on to the field at Comrade Stadium. The crowd numbered well over 80,000 and the noise they made seemed to underline for the Scots the pressure they were playing under as they strove to reverse the result of the first-leg match. The first forty-five minutes were hard fought with attack and counter-attack. Each side scored once, Albion's goal coming a minute from the break when Eric Cassidy turned a Frank Thomson cross into the net.

'You're doing well, boys,' said Jim Murray encouragingly, during the interval. 'Remember, they aren't good at coping with high crosses into their own penalty area.'

At the start of the second-half Albion pressed forward strongly and Bill Dawson hit the bar with a cracking shot in the third minute. Steadily, however, Abranov gained the upper hand and their striker, Anishenki, scored from close in with seventeen minutes gone on the large stadium clock.

Jim Murray turned to Doug. 'How is your leg?' The lad gulped. He so wanted to play, but if he went on to the field unfit, he could make things worse for the team. 'It seems okay, but I'm not sure.'

The manager made Doug do a few sprints up and down the touchline in his tracksuit, then looked at him quizzically. The teenager nodded. He felt no pain in the leg. Raising the number 13, Sam Barnet caught the referee's attention. Doug replaced Rob Malloy who had played well but was feeling the effects of a bad cold.

The youngster got into the action quickly, taking a pass from Ron Macleod and linking up with Taffy Rosser. A cross-field pass found Eric Cassidy whose cross was headed just wide by Fred Thomson. The play swept from end to end until, with only ten minutes left,

GOAL BEHIND THE CURTAIN

Doug intercepted a pass and broke down the right wing. Remembering Jim Murray's words he flighted a high cross to the vicinity of the penalty spot. Bill Dawson outjumped two Russian defenders to plant the ball firmly in the corner of the net.

The minutes ticked away as Albion, fighting the leg-weariness that seemed to clutch at them, mounted yet one more attack. Tom Pearson collected a thrown clearance from keeper Barrie and put Taffy Rosser away on a run. The Welshman weaved his way past two defenders before slipping the ball to Doug who crashed a great left-foot shot high into the net. The celebrations of the Albion players were cut short, however, by the referee's decision that the teenager had been offside.

Doug found himself tempted to protest the decision, which must have been extremely close, but from childhood days his father had impressed upon him the most basic tenet of the game – the referee is never wrong. As he faced up to the free kick Doug sensed it was all over for Albion. He felt sad, but reconciled himself to the disappointment by recalling that the little side from Dalkirk had done better than anyone could have anticipated. Furthermore, Doug could be well satisfied with the fact that well over 200 Bibles had been brought to needy Christians who might never have received them if Dalkirk Albion hadn't made it this far.

'God is no man's debtor.' The words flashed into the teenager's mind and they were accompanied with a strange urgency that made him chase Anishenki who was working the ball toward the Albion penalty area. Sliding into the tackle he dispossessed the skilful Russian, enabling Les Fernie to thump the ball downfield to Taffy Rosser, who held it long enough to let Eric Cassidy take up position near the Abranov's penalty box. The Irishman was forced out to the wing where he struggled hopelessly to get the ball on to his stronger left foot.

Doug had followed the play and was sprinting into the box when a despairing Cassidy swung his right foot at the ball. The stadium clock was counting the visitors out as Doug jumped to get on the end of what was a poor cross. It was the Russian centreback's ball all the way – until his own sweeper, jumping yards in front of him, mis-headed the ball completely, sending it neatly over the horrified defender to Doug who was already losing height when he got his head to the ball. It skipped over the diving keeper's groping hands, hit the post, and rolled over the line. Dalkirk Albion were into the final.

The dressing-room celebrations which followed seemed set to go on all night. Doug had been carried shoulder-high from the field by his team-mates. They had won a tie that had seemed to be running away from them right from the start of the first game in Scotland. They had had to fight to the finish to qualify, and that in itself was a valuable lesson to learn.

On board the team coach returning to their hotel the Albion players sang with delight, reminding the solemn Muscovites, unused to such displays of fervour, that there was a little country which still felt it ruled the world as far as football was concerned. They would have been much less enthusiastic however, had they known the sort of reception that awaited them at their hotel, for as they spilled out of the coach a number of tough-looking policemen closed in on them.

'Which one of you is Mackay?' asked the leader of the group.

Doug was already out of the coach by this time. 'Here I am,' he said.

The Russian lunged at the youngster and would

certainly have grabbed him, had one of his team-mates not stuck out a leg and tripped the man up. He went flying all his length.

'Run, Doug!' shouted a familiar voice, which the lad couldn't quite place at that moment. Without having a clue where he could run, Doug turned and fled, leaving the confused policemen to gather their wits and give chase. Quick as a flash he was round the corner and speeding into the night. But to his horror a car screeched to a halt just a little way ahead of him and the back nearside door opened. The teenager expected two policemen to jump out and give chase, but to his amazement a young girl, about his own age, leaned out of the door.

'Doug Mackay', she called, 'come in here.'

Who she might be Doug didn't know, but as he jumped into the car he was confident all was well, for the girl was holding up a Bible.

CHAPTER 10

TANYA

As the car sped through the streets of Moscow, Doug tried to collect his thoughts. Everything had happened so quickly that he found it hard to relate the events of the last fifteen minutes to each other. If the police (and customs officials) hadn't found the Bibles concealed in Hesperus why were they trying to arrest him? Surely not for knocking Abranov out of the Cup! And why had he run away? On the face of it that was the worst thing to do. Yet he had sensed he had to – that he would be in real danger if arrested. Never had he seen such anger as that which contorted the face of the policemen who had tried to arrest him; and what about these people in this car, threading its way through the back streets of the huge city? Who were they? Why did Doug trust them? How could they appear just in the nick of time like that?

As if she could read these questions in Doug's face, the girl sitting beside him spoke.

'My name is Tanya and these men in front of the car are my father and my uncle. We are members of the congregation which received the Bibles you brought.'

Tanya had a quiet reassuring voice which, together with her gentle features, convinced Doug that he was in the company of Christian people who had risked their own safety to protect him. Tanya continued her story, speaking in flawless English that suggested she had studied the language closely.

'Mr. Firth asked us to watch out for you, because he suspected that a member of your football club had some idea of what you were doing and was passing information to the communist authorities. We had someone inside the hotel to let us know if you needed help, and he was the man who informed us that there was a lot of police activity outside the hotel as the time drew near for your team bus to return from the stadium. He also told us something else. He saw one of your players watching your hotel room. Our man was quite sure of this for he also saw him looking at you with suspicion and dislike in the hotel lounge the night before the game.'

'Who could that have been?' gasped Doug.

'Our man didn't know his name. He was of average height, dark-haired and with blue eyes.'

Doug sighed: 'That description covers most of us,' he said. Then his eyes narrowed. He remembered one of his team-mates was a communist and therefore more likely than any other to oppose him. 'Simon Barrie,' he said tersely.

'It is never easy to be sure about such things,' broke in a voice from the front seat of the car. Tanya's uncle was speaking. 'The person who lets you down isn't always the person you suspect.'

At this point the car slowed down before turning right. They stopped at one of a number of lock-up garages belonging to a block of flats. As they locked up the garage and made their way to the flats, Doug realised they had shaken off the police who had been trying to pick up their trail. At last he felt he could relax. Tanya lived with her parents in a second-floor flat which was tastefully furnished and attractively decorated. The family welcomed the youngster warmly and he felt, as he had often done elsewhere, the real sense of friendship and trust there was between Christians. Here he was in a foreign country, hunted by the police, and yet he felt safe and happy.

Doug was very impressed by Tanya. She was nine-teen years old, the same age as himself, and yet she had the wisdom and experience of someone much older. As they ate a welcome meal Tanya told how she had been a member of the Communist Youth Organisation, the Komsomols, and had been very much opposed to Christianity.

'We were taught that religion was a hindrance to progress, keeping people poor and ignorant. I studied very hard at school, especially English language and literature, because I wanted to share the message of communism with the people of the West.'

Tanya went on to say that as she read English literature she saw more and more clearly how Western culture was based on the Bible.

'I had to read the Bible to see how you Westerners thought. Very soon I recognised that the Bible was special. It was like no book I had ever read. Christianity wasn't just for people in the West, but for all people. Truly, I realised, God must have given this Book to the world. I saw that Jesus Christ had died for me and I asked him to be my Saviour.'

At this point Tanya's voice broke, and it seemed as if she would start to cry. But she recovered and continued her story.

'I had been so bitter to Christians at school and now I was almost ashamed to come before the Lord, but he forgave me and helped me to encourage the young Christians I had once hurt so badly.'

At this point, Tanya's father spoke, telling Doug how their daughter's conversion had such a profound effect on them and on other members of the family, until one by one they too became Christians.

'Naturally, Tanya suffered for this in school. She left the Komsomols, and children who had once followed her admiringly became nasty to her and beat her up. Teachers who had formerly given her high marks in her subjects failed her and mocked her. But even some of them have been converted. God is blessing us so wonderfully.'

Doug was amazed to hear all this. No wonder Tanya seemed wise and mature, for she had come through so much in those four years since first she had come to faith in Christ. He was saddened to hear how she had been persecuted for her faith, to the extent that she was not even permitted to attend university. Doug could not help contrasting the wonderful freedom he himself enjoyed in his own land.

In the few days that followed Doug was able to tell Tanya and her family about his own experiences during the previous year. They were all thrilled to hear how God had been with him, and they chuckled as they listened to the amazing adventures of Hesperus the bear.

'I'll really miss him,' said Doug. 'If you find him give him a good home.'

It wasn't safe for Doug to remain too long in the flat. There was always someone ready to report to the authorities if a stranger was staying in the home of a Christian family. It would only be a matter of time until Tanya's parents had a visit from the dreaded KGB. In any case there was a means of escape to hand for Doug. Tanya's uncle, Georgi, was a lorry driver and that week he was due to drive to the small town of Grodno which was situated about ten miles from the Polish border. From there the young Scot, posing as a student, could hitch a lift into Poland, and on to West Germany – and freedom.

Naturally, Doug was keen to get on his way. His parents would be worried about him even although Mr. Firth would have been able to assure them he was safe for the time being. He was concerned about the publicity surrounding the case for the Russian newspapers were portraying him as a drug-smuggler and no doubt there would be anti-Christian people back in Britain who would be only too keen to believe that lie. At least the communist authorities would be left looking very silly when the truth came out. After all they claimed there was religious liberty for their people, yet they couldn't get Bibles unless these were smuggled in. When Doug got back home it could be very embarrassing for a lot of people.

One thing that concerned him was the effect of all this high drama on the players of Dalkirk Albion and especially on manager Jim Murray, whose new-found faith might be sorely tested by this development. Would he believe Doug was caught up in drug-smuggling? How would it affect the team's performance in the Cup Final? Weariness and stiff soccer opposition had all but beaten them in the quarter-final and the semi-final. Now, with one of their players lost in Europe, and the attention of the world's media on them, the pressure could prove too much.

Then there was Simon Barrie. How could he have been so low and despicable as to land Doug in this mess? Did he hate Christians so much that he grudged them Bibles? The really hurtful thing was that Doug had always felt Simon was honest. Argumentative, yes he was. Bad-tempered, even. But a traitor? Doug knew he must forgive Simon, for that is Christ's way, but he found himself stirred to bitterness and resentment every time he recalled what had happened.

At last Doug prayed: 'Lord, you kindly forgave me all my sins. As far as I can I forgive the person who has done this to me. Fill me with your forgiving love and clear out of me all feeling of anger.' That prayer was answered and the teenager found God's kindness and forgiveness really helping him win this battle that raged within.

When the day came for Doug to leave the Moscow

flat he felt a certain sadness. He had grown to like the whole family whose faith and kindness were such an encouragement to him. They had so many reasons to complain yet they thanked God for his goodness to them. They lived under many irritating, hurtful pressures, but these only made them brighter and more lovely in their Christian commitment. Most of all Doug knew he would miss Tanya. Her strong faith, her honest humility and her obvious gifts as a communicator suggested she would make an excellent missionary, yet she probably would not be allowed to leave her own country. Perhaps her whole life long she would be restricted to that city, living her Christian life in hostile surroundings. Even if that had to be, Doug was sure she would bring blessing into the lives of many.

'Good-bye, Tanya,' he said. 'We will pray for you often in Scotland. Maybe one day we will meet again on this earth.'

'Will you write to us?' asked Tanya quietly. 'You will get our address from Mr. Firth.'

'Of course I will,' said the youngster, adding with a smile, 'if I ever get home, that is.'

Even as he smiled, Doug knew the difficulty that faced him. He had thousands of miles to travel and two communist frontiers to cross. To add to his problems the Russian authorities were searching for him everywhere, aware that if he made it back to the West, it could expose them to international ridicule and contempt.

'If the authorities catch you they will have to make a big propaganda case of it. They will plant a huge quantity of drugs on you and give you a farce of a trial. You must be extremely careful,' said Tanya's father. Then he added with a smile, 'God has been with you all this time, he will not fail you now.'

He then produced a blonde wig, together with a thin

moustache and fitted them on to Doug. Tanya produced a camera and took a photograph, which developed quickly and was affixed to the passport papers they had prepared for the lad's journey home. 'You are Henry Currie, a student from Edinburgh,' laughed Tanya, handing Doug the papers which he placed in his own passport folder.

Tanya's father led them all in prayer, before Georgi and Doug slipped out of the flat and made their way, in the grey light of dawn, to the lorry that was to take Doug half-way to freedom. 'If I meet Hesperus, he won't recognise me in this disguise,' laughed the youngster.

It was a long journey covering hundreds of miles and two overnight stops at transport cafes. One evening, as they rested, Georgi brought Doug up to date with the news as he thumbed through the newspaper.

'You don't need to speak Russian to recognise this,' said Georgi solemnly, pointing to a photograph in the newspaper. It was Doug in his Dalkirk strip. He'd never been so unhappy to see his picture in the papers, especially when Georgi interpreted the caption that went with it: "Look out for this man". The young Scot shuddered, he felt as if everyone was looking at him and seeing through his disguise.

'Here's a bit of football news that will interest you,' said Georgi, desperate to find anything at all that would encourage Doug. 'Real Valencia of Spain will play Dalkirk Albion in the final of the U.E.F.A. Cup with the first leg in Spain and the second leg in Scotland. I think you will be back home in time to play in the final,' he added with a smile.

At that moment Doug felt as if he would never see the hills of home again. But before he went to sleep that night, he turned to the chapter he was reading from, Psalm 34. As he read verses 6 and 7 and turned them over in his mind, feelings of peace and confidence returned to refresh his spirit like a cool breeze on a hot day: *'This poor man cried and the Lord heard him, and saved him out of all his troubles. The angel of the Lord encamps around those who fear him, and delivers them.'*

Doug lay down and slept as peacefully as if he'd been in his own bed in the manse back in Dalkirk.

The next morning Georgi and his passenger were up at the crack of dawn to complete the last hundred miles of the journey to Grodno. They arrived about 11 a.m. and Georgi drove through the town to deposit Doug within ten miles of the border. As he got out of the cab, the youngster bumped his head slightly.

'Thank you so much, young friend, for all your help to us. We value these Bibles more than we can tell you, and although we are sorry for all the trouble you have had in Russia, at least it meant we were able to enjoy fellowship with you during the last week. That has been very special for us, and something I believe God brought to pass for our encouragement. I am sure you will get safely home. Pray for us as we will pray for you.'

A handshake, a smile, and he was gone – back to the hardship of being a Christian in the capital city of communism. It all seemed like a dream, yet that bump on the head reminded Doug he was very much in the real world of hard knocks and problems. In the distance Doug could see a big tanker coming toward him, heading for the Polish border. He hitched a lift, and to his relief, the tanker slowed down. 'I am travelling to Britain,' said Doug to the driver. 'Can you give me a lift, please?'

Clearly the man did not understand, but he opened the passenger door for the teenager to climb aboard. The driver was in a hurry and they soon reached the border. As they waited in a short queue at the border-crossing point, Doug noticed out of the side of his eye that the man seemed to be snatching furtive glances at him. Then he reached into the glove compartment and looked at something there. When the tanker itself reached the patrol point the driver grunted something to Doug and held up his finger, then jumped down from his cab. Doug assumed he wanted him to wait, but all at once he noticed, in the glove compartment, a copy of the newspaper he had seen the previous night in the cafe. To the youngster's horror he saw the paper was folded so as to reveal his photograph.

As he glanced up he caught sight of himself in the driving mirror. His hair-piece was askew revealing his own black hair protruding near his left ear. Doug realised at once what had happened. When he bumped his head climbing out of Georgi's cab he must have dislodged the hair-piece slightly. Georgi hadn't noticed this because when Doug stood at the driver's door saying farewell, it was the right side of his face rather than the left which Georgi had seen. However, when Doug sat in the second lorry it was the left side of his face that was to the driver all the time. The eagle-eyed driver had spotted something amiss and suspected that his passenger was indeed the runaway soccer star.

A glance confirmed Doug's worst fears. The border guards were hurrying toward him, accompanied by the driver. There wasn't a moment to be lost. Slipping into the driving seat of the tanker the lad released the brake and, using the clutch, engaged the gear. The engine changed tone and the huge vehicle hissed forward. The driver, purple with rage, shook his fist at Doug, but quickly jumped out of the way, landing in a ditch at the side of the road which was already occupied by two rather wet and angry border guards.

Doug raced up the gears as fast as the tanker would

respond. For all his fear of the consequences if he were caught, the teenager was enjoying this. It reminded him of his first time in the driving seat of a tractor, more than ten years ago on a Highland croft (with the owner's permission on that occasion). But this border road was no croft, nor was the rat-a-tat-tat of the guards' guns in any way like the barking of Frisky the collie pup who had been the companion of his boyhood adventures.

Most worrying of all this tanker was no five-miles-per-hour tractor and Doug was gaining speed rapidly, for by now the road was sloping gently downhill into Poland. The guards at the Polish checkpoint were taken so completely by surprise that they didn't even try to stop the runaway truck. By the time they were on their feet and into their car to give chase, Doug had disappeared round a corner, gathering speed at an alarming rate. This couldn't go on. Sooner or later a motorist coming in the opposite direction would be in serious danger. There was nothing else for it. Doug must give himself up.

It was easier said than done, however. To brake too suddenly now might cause the tanker to skid and make matters worse than ever. Doug prayed again: 'Lord, give me a way out? I look to you.' Suddenly, he saw an old road sloping gently upwards to the right. Using all his concentration and energy the teenager steered the tanker off the highway and up the disused track. This move took the guards so completely by surprise they overshot the entrance and had to continue until they found a turning point enabling them to renew the chase.

By this time Doug had reached the top of the narrow track and was able to see where it was leading. To his horror the road dipped sharply to reveal a gaping quarry surrounded by a fence that might well keep pedestrians back, but which would not restrain the tanker in any way. On the vehicle rolled gathering speed down the slope till it plunged over the edge, exploding in a terrifying ball of fire as it hit the quarry floor.

CHAPTER 11

THE WALL

The rhythmic wail of a siren roused Doug. A police car was nearby and drawing steadily closer. Slowly the reality of what had happened dawned on the boy. Seeing the yawning mouth of the quarry just ahead, and realising he couldn't hope to stop the tanker from plunging to the bottom he had pushed the door of the cab open and leaped from the doomed vehicle. The ground where he had landed sloped fairly sharply, and he had rolled fully twenty yards to land in a narrow ditch.

Doug's whole body was aching with the impact and each movement sent a stab of pain through him, but he realised he must try to move lest the police make a search of the area and find him. Lifting his head carefully he was able to see a strip of trees snaking westwards towards a village which he suspected would be Sokolka. There was a transport cafe there, and there, he felt sure, would be the passport to freedom, a lorry heading for Germany.

The teenager moved his arms and legs gingerly. Mercifully, nothing seemed to be broken, but he was very sore and knew it would take days for the bruising to clear up properly. The ditch he was lying in was dry and and extended, as far as Doug could see, for more than 200 yards down the side of the hill to the trees below. Gritting his teeth, Doug forced his protesting bones and muscles along the ditch, stifling a gasp of pain every few yards. He heard the car sirens grow louder then stop. Doors banged and voices spoke in loud and tense tones. The police had arrived. Soon they would search the area.

Doug battled on. He was relieved to notice that, in

spite of the impact when he had hit the ground, he did not appear to be bleeding. Doug thanked God for such a miraculous deliverance, for if there were no blood-stains there would be little or nothing to suggest to the police that he had survived the crash. The clamour of voices faded gradually into the background as Doug crawled on. Soon he came to the end of the ditch and found himself among the welcome shelter of the trees.

With a great effort Doug struggled to his feet and, leaning against a tree trunk for support, turned and gazed back up the hill. Clouds of black smoke were rising from the quarry, while the police struggled to restrain the gathering crowd of on-lookers. The quick-witted youngster saw at once that all this activity on the hilltop gave him the perfect opportunity to make his way unnoticed to the transport cafe.

What Doug hadn't counted on was the sheer dis-comfort of making such a journey in his bruised and battered condition. Every step was painful, and it seemed, as his pain-filled eyes looked through the trees toward Sokolka, that the village was moving away at the same weary pace as himself. Would he ever reach it? Darkness began to fall, and the chill of evening combined with pain and stiffness to make Doug feel thoroughly miserable. It was then he remembered his father's advice, 'When you feel downhearted, pray and sing.'

'Lord, help me,' he prayed. 'Give me the strength to go on? Get me to that transport cafe, and a lift to Germany?'

Having prayed, Doug started to sing. He didn't care that he might be overheard and reported to the police. There comes a time when praise must silence fear. He sang hymns he had heard as a child and choruses he had grown up with. His favourite was "All Will Be

Well" which had a tune that was easy for even Doug to
sing!

"Through the love of God our Saviour
All will be well.
Free and changeless is his favour;
All, all is well.
Precious is Christ's death that healed us,
Perfect is the grace that sealed us,
Strong the hand stretched forth to shield us;
All must be well."

The singing cheered Doug and at last he reached the
outskirts of the village. It was too dark to see very
much, but one thing was clear enough, the transport
cafe. It wasn't a large one but there were some lorries
parked outside, and Doug made his way quietly from
one to the other, taking care to keep out of sight of the
patrons seated by the window of the cafe. At last Doug
found what he was looking for – a large container
vehicle bound for Germany. He couldn't make out
the various words on the side, but the name
'DEUTSCHLAND' (Germany) was enough.

Doug tried the handle of the large door at the rear of
the vehicle and found, to his great relief that the door
was unlocked. It swung open to reveal, in the dim light
of the lorry-park, couches and settees of various styles
and sizes. 'It's a furniture van,' laughed Doug. 'Thank
you, Lord; this is the way to travel.' Doug climbed into
the van, pulling the huge door behind him until it
clicked shut. Struggling through the piled-up furniture
Doug found a long couch near the front of the van.
Taking off his shoes and jacket he stretched out, resting
his head on the low-lying arm of the couch, over which
he had draped his jacket for a pillow.

The teenager was utterly exhausted and within
minutes he was sound asleep. He didn't hear the driver
emerge from the cafe chatting to his co-driver, nor did

he hear him try the door of the van. The jolting movement of the truck didn't disturb him in the slightest. The events of the day had really taken their toll and Doug had never experienced such exhaustion. Time and again, during the journey of those last five miles, he had been so grateful for the tough training programme he'd undergone at Brickwell Stadium. Without it, he felt sure, he would simply have collapsed and had to give himself up. Now, at last, he could collapse in comparative comfort in the sure knowledge that God was keeping him safe.

How long he had been asleep Doug didn't know, but he was awakened by the sound of voices and the movement of furniture. The container van was stationary and the drivers were unloading its contents. Doug waited until he heard them move off carrying a couch, then he bobbed up his head to see where he was. It was still fairly dark, just before dawn as Doug guessed and they were in a side street in a city. Where the city was the lad couldn't tell. He was amazed to see that most of the furniture had already been unloaded. Just as well he had chosen to sleep right at the front of the van, and just as well he had woken up at that time.

Pulling on his shoes and tying them quickly, Doug grabbed his jacket and was heading for the door when he heard the voices of the removal men. They were returning. Doug tip-toed quickly back to the couch and hid behind it. The men were pulling the few remaining settees and couches towards the door of the van. Any moment now Doug would be discovered.

'Lord, stretch out your hand to shield me from view now?' The lad felt his hiding-place being pulled away and waited for the shout of surprise that would indicate he had been spotted.

That shout never came however. Doug looked up to see the removal man pulling the couch behind him by one hand over the back. He was looking towards the door talking to his companion who was obscured by the remaining settees grouped around the doorway. As long as the removal man didn't look round before jumping down on the roadway – he didn't. Soon their fading voices told Doug they were carrying a couch into the warehouse outside which they had stopped.

Doug thanked God for his protection, then crept to the doorway and looked cautiously. There was no one around so he jumped down from the van. The jolt made him gasp with pain. He was still bruised and sore. Quickly he crossed the road and headed for the main street ahead. Looking back as he turned the corner he saw the removal men busily unloading yet another couch. They had never seen their grateful passenger.

Where am I? What city is this? The questions perplexed Doug. One casualty of his last-moment exit from the tanker the previous day, had been his watch. A broken watch was no use and he had hidden it in the dense undergrowth near Sokolka. He couldn't see a clock anywhere that would give him an idea of the length of journey he had made. He was on the point of asking someone what the city was called, when he suddenly realised where he was. There on the right was a square and beyond that a large gate like the Arc de Triomphe. It was the Brandenburg Gate. Doug was stuck in communist East Berlin.

The youngster's heart sank. A short distance away was the dreaded Berlin Wall which encircled West Berlin, making it an oasis of freedom in a desert of oppression, for this divided city lay deep in the heart of communist East Germany and only the Western Sector which was administered by the British, French and Americans was free. The furniture van in which he had travelled from Poland had been an East German not a West German one. 'And I thought I was all right when I saw the word Deutschland,' said Doug to himself. 'Of all the places in Europe to end up, this must surely be the worst.'

The youngster sat down on a bench in the large square. He was cold, hungry and deeply discouraged. He felt he might as well have been sitting in Moscow's Red Square. How could he ever hope to get over that wall? He found bitterness mounting in his heart as he thought of the person who had betrayed him to the communist authorities. What a low down thing to do! Then Doug thought of the words of the New Testament: *"Bless those who curse you: bless and do not curse them"*.

Doug struggled with that command as he had never struggled with a Biblical statement before. He wanted to protest that what Simon Barrie had done was too bad ever to be forgiven, but he remembered how God forgives us our sins against him and we must forgive others. 'Help me, Lord. Please let your Holy Spirit fill me with forgiveness, for I don't feel very forgiving.' The lad prayed for a few minutes and gradually sensed the peace of God coming over him.

Praying didn't take the Berlin Wall away, but it helped Doug to realise that it might not be impossible to get beyond it. In fact, he found himself getting up and making his way to the Wall. Soon he was within sight of Checkpoint Charlie, the gate that marked the boundary between the two halves of the city. Pedestrians queued on the pavement to have their papers scrutinised by the guards, while those travelling by car were processed at a checkpoint on the roadway. Doug noticed that as the gate opened to let one car pass out of the Eastern Sector, so a gate some thirty or forty yards further on opened to let another car into the Western Sector. Once through the second gate, a man was free. The question was simple. Could a cold, hungry, bruised teenager run that distance in the short time the gates were open?

Doug joined the queue of pedestrians moving slowly up to the barrier. He tried to assess how long the gates were open for each car to pass through, but he found the time varied from as little as seven seconds to nearly twelve seconds. It would be touch and go for Doug. The minutes passed with agonising slowness, until he was up near the gate. Within the next sixty seconds he must make his move. He prayed quietly. Then, tensing his muscles, he was off. He sped past the astonished guard who was speaking to the driver of the next car in line.

By the time the guards had grasped what was happening, Doug was nearly half-way across the little stretch of no-man's land. Their shouts attracted the attention of the guards at the far end, one of whom moved to shut the gate while the other unslung his rifle menacingly. Doug put his head down and, bobbing from side to side, pulled every last ounce of effort from his aching, hungry body.

Suddenly a shot rang out. Doug was almost deafened as the bullet whistled fractionally past his ear. There was a yell of pain and the border guard crumpled to the ground holding his hand. Doug sped past him and was now only ten yards from the gate, which would certainly have been closed by this time had not a car stalled right in the middle of the checkpoint. The car had just moved off and the guard was desperately trying to slam the gate as Doug sprinted through.

As he collapsed with exhaustion he was helped by friendly bystanders. Seeing the state he was in they took him to a nearby cafe and gave him a welcome meal, before driving him to the British Consulate. As he thought about the events of the past hour it dawned on Doug just how near death he had been. The bullet that wounded the border guard in the hand had been aimed at his head – and missed by inches as he had weaved and ducked in his flight. Doug thanked God for his great escape.

When the British Consul discovered the identity of his new guest, he became very excited. 'We all thought you were dead,' he said. 'Killed when an oil tanker plunged into a quarry just inside the Polish border. The Reds were sure it was you.'

As Doug told his story, the Consul grew wide-eyed and open-mouthed with amazement. 'Did all that really happen?' he asked, a slightly envious tone in his voice, and a far-away look in his eyes. 'I say, what fun!' Then, as if coming back to reality, he added firmly, 'Of course, you will be very tired and you must rest, young fella.'

'Can I telephone my folks?' asked Doug. 'They'll be very upset if they heard that news about the tanker.'

The Consul put his hand on the lad's arm. 'That is what they will have heard, son. Better let me talk to them first.'

The Consul rang Doug's home and gently broke the good news. Doug could almost feel the silence at the other end of the telephone. Then he could hear his Mum crying. The Consul passed the receiver to him and he was able to speak. He told them very briefly how he had escaped and assured them he would be home next day. As they grasped the glorious truth that he was alive, they were beside themselves with delight.

'How good God is! How good God is!' Doug could hear his Dad repeating these words over and over.

The next day Doug flew into Glasgow Airport to be greeted not only by his delighted parents, but by television interviewers and pressmen. Doug answered their questions and told them something of his adventures. One press reporter asked if he regretted getting

involved in a problem so far away and 'interfering in
the affairs of another country'.

Doug replied simply, 'Did the Good Samaritan
regret "getting involved" in the affairs of a needy Jew?
Of course not. He was glad to help, whatever the cost.
As for "interfering in the affairs of another country", I
would give the same answer the apostle Peter gave to
the Jerusalem Council when they told him not to
preach about Jesus to the people. He said, "Whether it
is right in the sight of God to listen to you rather than
to God, you must judge; for we cannot but speak what
we have seen and heard".'

'I believe,' Doug went on, 'that since the earth is the
Lord's and everything on it, and since the powers that
rule are ordained by God, no government has the right
to withhold the Word of God from its people. I'm very
glad that a hundred more families now have Bibles
following my visit to the Soviet Union.'

The Press interview at an end, Doug and his parents
made their way to his father's car. Mr. Firth was waiting
there for them and he greeted Doug enthusiastically.

'That was wonderful, Doug. You've no idea what a
turmoil this has stirred up in Russia. The bad publicity
is making them think again about their policy of
making Bibles almost unobtainable. We must keep
praying things will change there.'

Doug was relieved to be home. It was only as he
began to unwind that he realised how tired he had been.
His body was still sore with bruising and his mind was
in a whirl with all the visitors he was receiving. He
wanted to rest and put the nerve-tingling adventure
behind him, but one question remained to be answered,
and that answer could only be found at Brickwell
Stadium. The staff and players of the club,
far from being angry with Doug's smuggling exploits,
were thrilled to have been indirectly involved in this

form of Christian espionage. Naturally, at first, when they were told one of their players had brought drugs into Russia, they were shocked and confused, but as the truth had come out so it led to widespread anger with the Russian authorities. Indeed, it had become a matter of national importance, and questions had been asked in Parliament.

Jim Murray had already called to see Doug at his home, but the players had respected his parents' wishes to give the lad some time to rest. As a result when he called at the ground, the players broke off training and gathered round him, glad to see him back.

'Great to see you, pal,' said Simon Barrie. 'You've done really well. Too bad you won't be fit for Wednesday in Spain.'

'Why did you do it, Simon?' asked Doug, looking him straight in the eye. 'Why did you betray me to the authorities?'

Doug saw the look of unbelief spread over the big goalkeeper's face, as his colour drained.

'Wha – what do you mean?' Simon stuttered.

'The Russian police were tipped off, just as the Romanian police had been back in October,' Doug went on. 'It was no accident they were waiting for us when we came off the coach outside our hotel. The Christians who picked me up saw a member of the team speaking with the police earlier and they were able to rescue me because they were keeping a protective watch on me.'

Simon Barrie looked totally mystified.

'Are you saying there's evidence to suggest one of the team shopped you?' asked Jim Murray grimly.

'No question,' replied Doug, 'and there's only one known communist amongst us – Simon.'

'It wasn't me, honestly,' said Simon. 'My communist ideas were shaken when you turned down the chance to sign for Morino. You could have been set up financially for the rest of your life and you turned it all down to follow Christ. I knew then that the Power of Christ is greater than the ideals of communism. I've been reading my Bible regularly for the last month – and – and – I've prayed a lot for you since that night you ran off after I tripped the Russian cop.'

Now it was Doug's turn to be surprised. 'So it was you who got in his way and let me escape. Well...er... thanks. Thanks so much. I'm sorry I thought it was you who put the police on me. Who could it have been?'

As Doug had been speaking there had been a nervous stirring at the back of the group of players. One man was feeling very uncomfortable.

'Doug, it...it was me. I did it.'

CHAPTER 12

FORGIVEN

'YOU did it, Ron!' gasped Doug. 'But why?'

'Well, I thought you were up to no good when I saw you leaving tartan cards around for certain people to see and leaving hotel-room doors open for visitors to go in with suspicious-looking sportsbags. Then there was that teddy-bear. It took me a while to grasp what you were doing, but at last I knew you were smuggling. I assumed it must be drugs and I saw it as a good chance to get even with you.'

'*Even* with me!' Doug broke in. 'Even with me for what? What have I ever done to you?'

Ron Macleod hung his head. Then he answered, 'When you first came here I noticed one or two things about you right away. First of all, you were confident without being the slightest bit big-headed. I guessed right away it must be your faith – a faith I don't have. I've always envied you that quiet confidence. I also saw you were a promising player. Very quickly you improved and I realised you were better than me – me, the only international at Brickwell Stadium at that time. I found it very hard to accept. Jealousy is a terrible thing. It has a logic all of its own. The jealous man always feels that he is right and the person he hates is wrong. If that hated person actually does something wrong you want to make him pay for it.'

Doug could hardly believe his ears as Ron continued.

'Jealousy drove me to hate you, and when I suspected you of smuggling drugs I felt sure I could finish your football career and expose you as a hypocrite at the same time. When I realised it was Bibles you were carrying into these countries, I felt ashamed of my attitude for the first time; but by then you were in hiding in Russia. Now that you're back I'm glad you're safe. It's been on my conscience that you could have been killed, and I'm glad that you and everybody else knows about it now. It's a relief to have it all out in the open.'

Macleod turned towards the dressing-room leaving the Albion squad in stunned disbelief.

'Wait a minute, Ron.' It was Doug speaking. 'All's well that ends well. No hard feelings.' Doug held out his hand and the internationalist shook hands before hurrying off to change.

Jim Murray shook his head sadly. 'Aye, he had a great career in front of him.'

'Had?' echoed Doug. 'Surely his career isn't over yet?'

The manager looked at him in surprise.

'I was just thinking', the youngster explained, 'that if Ron could play so well for Albion with all that jealousy locked up inside him he should be even better now that he has confessed it and got rid of it.'

Jim Murray had a strong feeling that Macleod should be made to pay for his nastiness to Doug, which after all could have cost the boy his life, but maybe Doug's forgiving attitude was right. The manager would have to think about it and pray about it. Although his own faith had been shaken when Doug disappeared, the overall effect of the lad's adventure had been to convince the manager that God could be trusted.

Doug still wasn't match-fit when the team was announced for the game with Real in Valencia. He was allowed to stay at home and catch up on his studies so that he could be prepared for the forthcoming examinations as well as completing projects and other assignments.

The match did not go well for the Scots. Two goals

down at half-time, they had missed a second-half penalty. Skipper Wallace Thain had crashed his kick against the post and, to make matters worse, Real had collected the rebound and dashed up-field to score what appeared to be a decisive goal, as it left Albion needing to score four goals in the second leg to win the Cup.

In the meantime, Doug was in demand all over the country, as churches and other groups wanted to hear more about his exciting experiences behind the Iron Curtain. For the most part he refused. Time was short and he regarded his university studies as part of his call from God. Though he couldn't see the way ahead all that clearly, he knew he must use his time wisely, completing his course with the best degree pass he could obtain. However, one day he received a letter which made him realise he needed to put his story into print. The letter was from Tanya, and in it she told him how big an impact Doug's adventures had made on the people of Moscow, especially the youth.

To his surprise the young Scot found that far from resenting his intrusion, most people saw it as an act both of daring and caring. He had taken great risks and taken them for ordinary Russian people. Tanya urged Doug to tell of his exploits as widely as possible so that as many people as possible might learn about the conditions she and young people like her were living under. Perhaps then more people would pray for changes to take place. Doug made up his mind to put the matter in hand as soon as his exams were over.

When Jim Murray announced his team for the second game with Real Valencia, there was a place for Doug in the centre of the midfield. 'Things won't be easy, lads,' the manager told his men. 'We have got to score at least four goals. But it isn't impossible. The whole country is behind you, and Real will be apprehensive about coming here. They know that if they lose an early goal they could be in trouble for the rest of the game. Just keep cool, and remember the tactics we've gone over in training.'

It was a lovely May evening which welcomed the two sides on to the lush Brickwell turf. The ground was packed to capacity and the presence of television cameras guaranteed an audience of millions. Albion's team was along the usual lines:

Simon Barrie in goal; Les Fernie at right back and Norrie Harvey at left back. In the centre of the defence was Tom Pearson, partnered by skipper Wallace Thain. Ron Macleod and Rob Malloy were playing with Doug in the midfield, one on either side of him. The Albion attack was made up of Taffy Rosser on the right wing, Bill Dawson playing through the middle, and Eric Cassidy on the left wing.

Albion lost the toss and kicked off, but were under pressure within minutes as Real pressed forward in search of an early goal that would surely have taken the U.E.F.A. Cup back to Spain. Del Sol, their brilliant striker, gave both Pearson and Thain the slip before firing a tremendous drive from about twenty yards. That shot was bound for the back of the net until Barrie threw himself to his right and clutched it. The crowd roared their approval of a fantastic save. Better was to follow, however, for Barrie, having held on to the ball long enough to cool the game down, sent a prodigious kick deep into Real's half. Bill Dawson rose as if to head it, then ducked and side-stepped so that the ball bounced through to Eric Cassidy, who out-jumped the Spanish defence to head the ball in the direction of Taffy Rosser. The winger pounced and was dribbling towards goal when he was upended unceremoniously by Real's sweeper, Jose Andera.

Referee Marcel from France waved away the

FORGIVEN

Spanish protests and pointed firmly to the penalty spot. Skipper Wallace Thain placed the ball on the spot and walked back before beginning his run. He had missed a penalty in the first leg and that had cost Albion dearly; but if he missed this one they would almost certainly be out of the competition altogether. He had wanted to leave any penalties there might be that night to someone else, but manager Jim Murray had insisted Wallace take them himself, knowing the skipper needed a boost to his confidence. Thain started his run. He belted the ball, and although keeper Pedro guessed correctly where the kick was going, he could only help it into the net.

Wallace Thain leaped delightedly in the air, as his team-mates thronged around him. It was a perfect start, for not only did it inspire the home team it shook Real's confidence, making them adopt a dour defensive style of play for the next thirty minutes. Gradually Doug and his midfield colleagues took more and more control of the game. It was becoming one way traffic and keeper Pedro was called into action over and over again. Only his brilliance kept the Spaniards in the game.

Even Pedro, however, could do nothing to prevent Albion's second goal. A free kick by Les Fernie was helped on by Ron Macleod to Eric Cassidy who had his back to the goal, about fifteen yards out. Falling back, the Irish lad did a dramatic overhead kick which sent the ball high into the back of the net. The Dalkirk crowd danced on the terracing. Victory looked a distinct possibility now. Pressing forward Albion hoped to wipe out Real's goal advantage by the interval, but in their enthusiasm they left themselves open to a smart counter-attack.

Manfred, Real's German midfield man sent a clever pass forward to Del Sol who back-heeled to Sebastian.

111

His pass in turn found Manfred speeding forward. Rounding Tom Pearson, the German picked out Del Sol just inside the penalty area and the Spanish striker gave Simon Barrie no chance.

It was the Albion players who were relieved to hear the half-time whistle, for that goal, coming when it did, had really disheartened them. Jim Murray had a huge task on hand trying to lift his players during the brief interval. He knew the problem that faced them. Three goals in forty-five minutes against a team of this calibre was a tall order. As he headed down the tunnel to the dressing-room the manager prayed simply: 'Lord, give me the words to say to lift these lads for the second half?'

Once inside, Jim Murray got the Albion players seated quickly and began to speak to them. 'You're well able to win this match,' he said. 'The first half was yours. You were all over them as long as you played with a bit of method, but once you began to rush at them they caught you out. Remember, be thinking what you are going to do with the ball before it comes to you. That way you are a step ahead of your opponents.'

By the time the interval was over the home team were in a far more competitive frame of mind, and they quickly took control.

Doug ran thirty yards, evading two tackles, before finding Norrie Harvey with a neat pass. The English lad sent a high ball through to Bill Dawson who nodded it down for Rob Malloy to shoot for goal. Rob's shot cannoned off Andera and bounced back to Malloy, who passed it infield to Doug. Before the Real defenders could close him down Doug touched the ball up with his right foot and crashed it left-footedly into the net. It was the best 'bicycle kick' the lad had ever done and it completely foxed the goalkeeper. Dalkirk

FORGIVEN

Albion were back in the game once more.

The men from Valencia defended stoutly and it took Dalkirk fully twenty more minutes to score again. Les Fernie collected a throw from keeper Barrie and made ground on the right before passing infield to Ron Macleod. The internationalist dummied the ball letting it run through to Doug, who sped past two Spanish defenders and lobbed the ball to Taffy Rosser on the right wing. This sudden change of tempo in the build-up caught the visitors off-guard and Rosser was able to sprint to the bye-line unchallenged before crossing the ball for Bill Dawson to head home.

The crowd cheered and cheered. The Real team argued amongst themselves, and the Albion players encouraged one another to give it all they had for the remaining twenty minutes. Jim Murray sent on both his substitutes in the hope that their freshness would put even more pressure on the Spaniards, but the visitors were desperately trying to retain possession of the ball and frustrate Albion. Doug had noticed that some of Dalkirk's best moves had started with goalkeeper Simon Barrie, so the next time he saw him holding the ball, Doug ran into a space and shouted. Simon threw the ball to him and he trapped it.

'Look out, Doug,' shouted Tom Pearson. The lad moved quickly to his left and rolled the ball back sharply with the sole of his boot. Del Sol who had been charging in to tackle him was left to go rushing harmlessly past, whilst Doug set off on a run, to the accompaniment of a swelling cheer of anticipation from the crowd. Doug shuffled past one opponent and drew the challenge of another before slipping the ball to Bob Allan, who had come on as a substitute. Allan drove forward but was quickly closed down by two Spanish players. Seeing Doug just ahead he stabbed the ball through to him.

GOAL BEHIND THE CURTAIN

The teenager was now over the half-way line, with three defenders barring the way to goal. Eric Cassidy was to Doug's left and, as the Real full-back Moringue slid towards him, he touched the ball to Eric and ran on. Through came the return pass, but at the last moment he shimmied, let the ball run through his legs and ran on. The move caught the Spanish centre-back completely off balance, and now Doug was faced only by Jose Andera.

Feinting left, Doug swung right to shake off the wily Spaniard. Just then a voice rang out. 'Pass it quickly, Doug.' Looking up, the lad saw Ron Macleod coming up on his right. Something instinctively made Doug want to go it alone and he swerved to the left. But, just as he was about to sweep past Andera, he felt a check in his spirit. Swaying back again, Doug shoved the ball forward, to his right. The pass was perfect and Ron Macleod, fastening on to it, struck the ball firmly. It never rose off the ground until it rebounded from the stanchion holding up the net, hit the back of the diving goalkeeper, and cannoned back into the net.

It was a goal worthy of winning any cup final and the crowd cheered it to the echo. Ron Macleod disappeared under a mass of jubilant players. They had struggled through so much to this point and, with only a few minutes left, they knew they had won. So did Real Valencia for they offered only a token resistance until the final whistle blew. In spite of loudspeaker appeals for order, hundreds of young fans poured on to the field and the presentation ceremony was delayed until they could be shepherded back to the terracing.

At last it was time for the presentation. Real received their runners-up medals and also the warm applause from the crowd which their sporting play deserved. Then the U.E.F.A. Cup was presented to Wallace Thain with a few well-chosen words by the official who had travelled from Austria for the occasion. The noise was incredible as Wallace Thain held the trophy aloft. How often throughout the season the task of winning it had seemed to be beyond them, and yet the dream had come true.

'You didn't need to give me that pass, Doug,' said Ron Macleod. 'You could probably have gone through and scored yourself.'

Doug shook his head emphatically. 'That one had your name written all over it,' he said; adding with a twinkle in his eye, 'that daisy-cutter was straight enough to win the open at St. Andrews.'

'They're calling for you,' said Ron, nodding to the packed terracing and stand.

Sure enough, the crowd were chanting Doug's name. He waved to them, acknowledging their encouragement and then set off on the customary lap of honour with the whole squad, showing off the cup to the accompaniment of cheers and handclapping. But to Doug's embarrassment, the chanting of his name started up again and continued, until Mr. Delaney, the club chairman stepped forward.

'I think you should take the microphone, Doug, and say a few words to them.'

The boy went red in the face. 'I can't do *that,* sir.'

But the microphone was in his hand and Mr. Delaney was walking back to rejoin the other officials. The crowd roared their approval and shouts of 'SPEECH, SPEECH!' swept round the stadium. Doug bowed his head in a brief word of silent prayer, for he needed God's strength now.

'When I first ran on to this pitch to play for the Albion,' Doug began, 'I felt nervous and shy. When I kicked my only penalty here against Wallachia I was shaking, but these moments were nothing compared to this – talking to a congregation of 20,000. That's as many people as my Dad speaks to in a year.'

The happy laughter of the crowd eased the tension which the youngster felt. It was just as well he had forgotten about the television cameras, beaming his impromptu words to millions. That might have been too much for him to cope with.

'This has been a great season for us as a club – one we'll always remember, and today crowns it all. But it's been a special year for me. For another reason, because...because, during this time I've come to know God in a deeper way than ever before. I never could have imagined that I would be guided to bring Bibles to hundreds of people in Eastern Europe. I never dreamed I would be interrogated, hunted and shot at. Yet, through it all I've learned a great lesson – God loves me and I can trust him far more deeply than I ever imagined.

'When I was a child I trusted the Lord to be my Saviour, to forgive me my sins and save me from hell. Now I'm learning to let my Saviour lead me and be truly the Lord of my life. I don't know what lies ahead for me, but I trust the One who does know. His way is best for me and his way is best for you too. The Bible tells us that one day there will be another presentation ceremony, when God's people who have trusted and served him will be presented with rewards by him. Then he will say to each of them: "Well done, good and faithful servant, enter into the joy of your Lord".

'What a glorious moment that will be. All the struggles we've had, all the hurts we've suffered, all the things we've been through will be worth it at last when we are safely with the Lord. Will you be there? Are you following the Lord Jesus Christ? He has promised us all, "you will find me when you search for me with all your heart"!

'God bless you all!'

FORGIVEN

The huge crowd was silent as Doug handed back the microphone, then there was the sound of singing. It was quiet at first:

'Amazing grace how sweet the sound,
   That saved a wretch like me;
   I once was lost, but now I'm found,
   Was blind but now I see.'

Quickly, the singing spread until the whole crowd was joining in:

'When we've been there ten thousand years
   Bright shining as the sun,
   We've no less days to sing God's praise
   Than when we first begun.'

As the song ended, the crowd broke into prolonged cheering and applause.

* * * * *

Now, by the Berlin Wall, another crowd was singing and cheering. They were free. For some it was freedom from the fear of invasion by a Communist Army, or freedom from worry about relatives in East Berlin – relatives they had scarcely seen for decades. For others it was freedom from restrictions placed on their movements, their activities and their words. The faces of all of them radiated supreme happiness.

As Doug watched them he thought again of Tanya in Moscow, and the young kit attendant with F.C. Wallachia, the boy who had been so happy to receive one of the Bibles Doug had smuggled into Romania. Stepping forward he picked up a piece of stone that had been knocked off the hated wall by a bull-dozer. Taking a marker pen from his coat pocket he wrote on the stone the words: 'If the Son shall make you free you shall be free indeed.'

Bending down, Doug put his arm around young

117

GOAL BEHIND THE CURTAIN

Richard's shoulders and placed the stone in his hand.

'You are free, little chap,' he told the boy. 'Free to grow up learning of God and loving God. May he bless you to serve him one day, and to help others find him as their Lord. Keep this stone. Remember, just as God is knocking down that wall in front of your eyes, so he will finally knock down every barrier that hinders you from serving him. Have faith in God. He will never let you down.'

Doug gave the wee boy a cuddle, then he straightened up and embraced Mikhail.

'The Lord bless you, in your work for him, brother,' said Doug. 'There's still much to be done for the sake of the gospel in Eastern Europe. But now you're free – and you have the Bible. That always was our goal behind the Curtain.'

THE END

ONLY   CHILDREN

Anne   Rayment

Joey has problems as a fourteen year old Christian.

His parents are divorced and his father has remarried.

Joey stays with his mum, but idolises his father who invites him to stay for a while.

Joey is fond of Camilla, who belongs to a strange cult.

Then Emma, a school friend, disappears after being befriended by Camilla.

How does Joey and his sister, Sarah, aged twelve, react to all this? What about Sophie, a Christian the same age as Joey?

for 11-15 years

160pp   pocket paperback

ISBN1 871676 290

A
DIFFERENT MARY

Anne Rayment

Christian novel based on a character called Mary.

She is thirteen, from a broken home, and is rejected by her mother. However she meets the Fellows family and their friends at Gladstone Street Baptist Church.

A very topical story, well written and easy to read.

for 10-14 year old girls.

196pp   large paperback

ISBN O 906731 95X

THE
WHITE   STONE

Pauline   Lewis

Biblical novel set in the time of Solomon.

Michael's father is unwell and in danger of losing his property. Yet at one time he was a friend of the young prince, Solomon: even saving his life.

Read how Michael diligently tries to gain access to King Solomon's palace and how the wise king deals with the problem.

for 10-15 years

80pp   ISBN 1 871676 207   pocket paperback

THE
HIGH HILL

Pauline   Lewis

Biblical novel set in the time of Elijah with its central event being the encounter between Elijah and the prophets of Baal on Mount Carmel. The story is about Nathan and Anna who know that one day they will be married since it has been arranged by their respective parents.

Read how their faith in God is tested in these stirring times.

for10-15 years

80pp   ISBN 1 871676 142   pocket paperback

The Sarah and Paul Series
by
Derek Prime

In this set of pocket paperbacks, read how nine year old twins, Sarah and Paul Macdonald, discover answers to important questions when their parents help them to understand the Bible.

GO BACK TO SCHOOL
Discover about *the Bible and about God*
80pp   ISBN 1 871676 185

HAVE A VISITOR
Discover about *the Lord Jesus Christ*
80pp   ISBN 1 871676 193

GO TO THE SEASIDE
Discover about *the Holy Spirit* and *the Church*
80pp   ISBN 1 871676 345

MAKE A SCRAPBOOK
Discover about *The Lord's Prayer*
80pp   ISBN 1 871676 355

GO TO THE MUSEUM
Discover about *The Ten Commandments*
96pp   ISBN 1 871676 363

ON HOLIDAY AGAIN
Discover about *Becoming a Christian*
96pp   ISBN 1 871676 371